the Whole Sky

HEATHER HENSON

A Caitlyn Dlouhy Book

Atheneum Books for Young Readers

atheneum   New York   London   Toronto   Sydney   New Delhi

atheneum

ATHENEUM BOOKS FOR YOUNG READERS

An imprint of Simon & Schuster Children's Publishing Division

1230 Avenue of the Americas, New York, New York 10020

The Simon & Schuster Speakers Bureau can bring authors to your live event.

For more information or to book an event, contact the Simon & Schuster Speakers Bureau

at 1-866-248-3049 or visit our website at www.simonspeakers.com.

Interior design by Tom Daly

Jacket design by Lauren Rille and Tom Daly

The text for this book was set in Adobe Caslon Pro.

Manufactured in the United States of America

0717 FFG

First Edition

2 4 6 8 10 9 7 5 3 1

CIP data for this book is available from the Library of Congress.

ISBN 978-1-4424-1405-1

ISBN 978-1-4424-1407-5 (eBook)

For my sister, Holly Henson,
and for my friends
David Campbell and Annie Leah Sommers,
in loving memory

The sky is everywhere,
even in the dark beneath your skin.

—from "Sky"

by Wisława Szymborska,
View with a Grain of Sand

Part One

Things Sky had always known:

A pinch of salt tossed over the left shoulder will blind the devil's eye and drive his mischief away.

A horseshoe hung upright above a door will catch the luck and hold it true—at least until the horseshoe tips.

An eyelash loosed upon your cheek can carry a wish—*if* you hurry and swipe the lash along the back of your hand, close your eyes, and stick your arm straight out. And *if* the lash gets whisked away of its own accord.

Sky's father would laugh or wink when telling about the old superstitions, the old ways he'd learned from his granny when he was just a young boy back in Ireland, and yet he seemed to know them all.

A black cat walking toward you is a good thing, but a black cat walking away is a whole different story.

A bird trapped inside a kitchen means a death is coming.

A hat tossed upon a bed is trouble always, and an old broom brought to a new home will never, ever sweep the place clean.

Sky knew her father was never above rapping at a piece of wood to guard against even the hint of bad luck. And he was always reaching up to rub a thumb and forefinger to the old St. Christopher medal worn forever around his neck.

"Better to be safe than sorry," he'd say if he caught her looking. "Better to be safe than sorry, Sky, my luv." Piling on the Irish brogue when he wanted to, spreading it thick, though most times the accent barely tinged his words. He'd left Ireland when he was ten.

And of course the world Sky and her family moved through, most of the people they knew—breeders, owners, and trainers; jockeys and grooms—people in the business of horses, accepted the hard fact that luck can change in the flick of a tail. And it was usually a given that once bad luck had found you, it could cling like smoke from a cigarette; it could follow wherever you might go.

1

Just a small wooden sign here; blink and you'd miss it.

SHAUGHNESSY FARMS

Nothing like out front. With the big stone pillars to mark the entrance. And the wrought iron gate with the name woven through in delicate curlicue. With the historic plaque announcing Shaughnessy's place as one of the finest Thoroughbred broodmare farms in Kentucky.

No, this was the back entrance—employees only—and Sky's father slowed enough to make the sharp turn, bringing the truck and trailer to a hard stop at the locked gate.

"Smile for the camera," he said, an old joke, then did the opposite, frowning at the digital eye perched near the buzzer.

It took a while, but finally a voice Sky knew better than just about anybody's came out, garbled and crackling, from the speaker.

"'Bout time, James Doran! Two weeks late, and no word at all! I'll dock your pay for that."

"And I'll dock your head, Frank Massey. Let us in!"

The gate swung slowly open, like magic, Sky had always thought when she was little, the whole place seeming like a magic storybook kingdom filled with the most beautiful creatures ever made.

Allah breathed, and his breath became the horse—that's what it said in the book of Arabian horse legends her mother had read to her every night a few summers ago, and that's what she nearly believed. Allah is God in Arabia, her mother had explained, and Sky used to imagine that the first horse ever was made that way, from nothing but air and spirit. She could almost imagine it still.

But now she was ready to see the real thing again. More than ready, after months and months, and all she'd been through, she was aching, starved. So the minute the truck made it through the Shaughnessy gate, she had the seat belt off, the window down, and she was leaning most of the way out.

"Careful," her father warned, but he was barely doing twenty, taking it all in himself.

The land, the way it rolled, soft and sweet. Not too flat in any one place, not too steep either. No weeds along the fencerows; not a single blade of grass out of place. Long black boxes of barns dotting the pastures. And miles and miles of four-planked wooden fence.

The fence was hunter green instead of white or black like most fancy horse farms. The green made Shaughnessy stand out from all the others; the green made something puff up inside Sky's chest every time she saw it. As if she owned the whole place and all the million-dollar mares kept within the green barrier—a few of which she was finally seeing, farther off than she'd hoped for a first look, but a sight for sore eyes just the same. Glossy red coats shimmering in the sun, legs as long as a year. Gorgeous.

Sky couldn't talk to horses from this far away, but she started buzzing anyway. Her whole body. Buzzing like their old electric teakettle after it had been plugged in but hadn't started boiling yet.

And she knew without looking back over her shoulder, knew that her father was the same. Because that's the way it was with the two of them, always had been, for as long as Sky could remember.

2

For Sky, talking to horses wasn't talking exactly. Not like "Hi, there, how are you?" "Oh, I'm fine, thank you very much." It was more like knowing. Like touching something and knowing what it feels like, inside and out.

The knowing used to scare her, the way it would come on so strong and fast.

When Sky was just a baby, she'd be with her father inside a barn somewhere, happy as a beagle one minute, bawling her head off the next. Because the horse was telling her something, and she wanted to help, but she couldn't even talk yet herself.

"What's wrong with your girl, James?" people would ask. "Is she scared of horses? Oh, that's a shame! With you such a horseman and all."

Later, when she could talk, those same people would just

stare at her after she'd told them how their horses didn't like the cheap feed they'd been given or how they didn't fancy being cooped up in a stall all week only to be ridden out on a Sunday.

"And how would you know that, little miss?"

"The horse told me."

"The horse told you!" A great big laugh. "Your daughter's got real imagination, doesn't she, James?" Repeating it till everybody in the barn was laughing. "'The horse told me.' Did you hear that?" Winking at Sky. "Why, of course he did, young lady!"

At first she didn't understand.

"What's wrong with them, Dad? Why don't they listen?"

"They don't know how."

"But I hear the horses, I hear them. . . ."

"I know you do."

"Then why can't everybody?"

"It's something you're born with, or not."

"And we are?"

"Yes."

"Why?"

"Well, that's like asking why you were born with black hair and dark eyes to match. Even in a family full of red-heads. It's something that got passed down. From me, from my granny. From those who came before."

"But why can't we—"

"It's a gift, Sky," he interrupted, getting to the heart of it. "Something our particular family's always had, going way back. One per generation. But it's a secret we keep to ourselves. A bit of it we share—to make a living, to do what we love. But the whole thing we never tell." He tapped a finger lightly to her chest. "We keep the secret here, always."

And so Sky had learned to keep the secret hidden long ago. But that's not all she was holding on to that foaling season.

"You've got to be strong, Sky," her mother had said before she died two short months ago. "You've got to be extra strong. For your dad."

And so she was keeping the sadness hidden too. Way down deep, buried along with the secret and another thing she couldn't quite put a name to. But it didn't matter. Everything was locked tight inside her now, and she would be strong this foaling season, strong no matter what.

3

James Doran didn't stop the truck to greet the first herd of far-off mares like he usually did, and Sky's heart sank just a little as she watched the perfect creatures disappear again.

"Frank'll be clocking us," he said, though Sky hadn't made a peep.

Sure enough, as soon as they turned into the foaling barn parking lot, there he was, the old man. Standing stiff as a jailer, a deep scowl slashing his face.

Sky gave a snort; she couldn't help it. The harsh look would've been a whole lot more convincing if it weren't for the dog. Burley was his name—it's the type of tobacco grown in Kentucky, the leaves going rich and brown when they're dried. Rich and brown like the dachshund's coat, though his face was nearly white now.

Burley was standing roly-poly and glued to Frank's left ankle like always. Wagging his curved stick of tail so hard at the sight of their truck, it was like the stick was wagging the dog.

"Now's our chance!" her father said, making a big show of heading straight for the old man, like he was going to run him down, swiping the wheel to the right in time, stomping on the brakes.

"Can't get rid of me that easy, James Doran!" Frank called. He slapped the younger man—hard—on the back as soon as he came out of the driver's side, then gave him a rough hug.

"And who's that you got with you?" he said as Sky hopped out of the truck. "Can't be Sky, no sir. That gal's too big!"

"Yep, it's me." Sky glanced down at her boots, saw that her ankles were showing. She needed new pants, new shirts—everything had seemed to shrink in the last few weeks. Her mother would need to take her shopping soon—the thought came before she could stop it. And she bit down hard on the inside of her right cheek, a raw place already, fresh with blood, to numb what would come next: the certain and terrible knowledge that her mother was never going to take her shopping ever again.

"Lord have mercy," Frank was saying, "she's taller than me!"

"Ah, well, that's no surprise." Her father rested a hand

atop the old man's snowy white head. "A three-year-old's taller than you."

"And I can still take you down a notch!" Frank slapped the hand away. "Don't think I can't."

Frank Massey had been a jockey back in the day. He was small but wiry strong. Stringy and tough like beef jerky, he'd tell you himself. He'd been training horses and managing Shaughnessy just about forever.

"How old are you now, girl?" Frank squinted over, and Sky made a face, knowing he was just pretending to forget.

"Twelve."

"Twelve, is it?" He clicked his tongue. "Ah, well, twelve's not too old for a hug, so come on over, what are you waiting for, don't have all day!"

Sky moved to do as she was told. A quick, gruff hug like always, she was thinking. But this time Frank held on longer, and when she looked, she saw how his sharp blue eyes had gone all watery. She stumbled backward a bit, turning and kneeling down to fuss over Burley—all to stop the water from pooling up in her own eyes.

A few drops'll bring a flood.

That's what her mother used to say. And Sky wasn't going to start off soggy her first day back to Shaughnessy, she'd promised herself that.

"I got the foaling barn cleaned out since you weren't here to do it." Frank's voice cracked. He grabbed a red hanky from his back pocket, swiped at his eyes, his nose. Cleared his throat. "Fifty-two this year—same as last, give or take."

Her father had looked away from the old man, but he gave a knowing nod. Fifty-two mares foaling in one season was standard for Shaughnessy. The farm was still family owned so it was a relatively small Thoroughbred operation. Corporate farms—ones with big business co-owners and boards of directors—could have up to three hundred Thoroughbred mares foaling over a two-month stretch.

"So, first thing in the morning, you got to bring all the early mares into the foaling barn," Frank continued. "You're cutting it close, sure enough. A mare needs time to settle into a new stall before she'll feel easy 'bout birthing her foal!"

"You telling me my business, old man?"

"Stopped doing that long ago."

"Could've fooled me."

The needling each other, the rough joking, it was all part of how Frank and James Doran communicated, and Sky was used to it. In fact she was counting on it.

"Come on, then." Frank clapped his hands together.

"Let's get you two unloaded, haven't got all day."

Sky hurried to follow orders, but the sound of hoofbeats moving fast, moving closer, made her stop and look toward the pasture.

Frank whistled. "That's sure a welcoming committee if ever I saw one."

"The best," Sky whispered, because it was true. There was nothing better than a bunch of horses rushing at you, drawn by the sound of your truck, the deep knowledge of who you are, a need to get to you fast.

"Hey, Marigold, hiya, Penny! Hey, Floss!" Sky started calling out their names as she went to the paddock fence, stepping up on the first plank, reaching her arms full out as if she could catch and hold the whole entire herd. "Hello, Miss Lynn. Hey there, Darsha. Hiya, Dulcimer!"

The mares slowed to a joyful trot, and as soon as they were near enough, they were answering back, horse thoughts zinging into Sky's head.

How glad they were to see her—and her father of course, when he came up to the fence. How much they'd missed them both. Some of the mares started in right away, telling her father all about their aches and pains, minor slights in the barn.

"Hold on, give us a chance, ladies!" James laughed, a real

laugh, Sky noticed, first time in forever. "We've only just gotten here!"

Some of the mares started nipping and nudging, jostling each other for a closer spot near the fence.

"Careful now," James scolded, gentle but firm. "Careful."

Lady Blue—the leader, the boss of this particular herd of mares—came sashaying through, big belly swaying like a boat at sea. Sky leaned over the fence and put her palm flat against the swollen middle.

"He's a big 'un, don't you think?" Frank said.

"Big," she agreed. "But who says it's a 'he'?"

Frank was the only one, what with Sky's mother gone, the only one in the whole world who knew what she and her dad could do. Most people just assumed they had a way with horses and left it at that.

"What do you think?" Frank asked her now. "Colt or filly?"

"Not sure," Sky answered, wishing she knew, wishing she and her father could talk to the foals inside their mama's bellies. But they never could. The unborn foals stayed silent until the moment they slid out into the straw.

"Ah, well, we'll know soon enough," Frank said, and then he looked to her father. "Don't know why you cut it so close getting here. I kept calling, trying to find out when you were coming. When I didn't hear from you—"

"Phone died." James interrupted, and Sky felt her stomach clench.

It was a lie—or mostly a lie. She'd listened to the phone herself, listened to it ring and ring and ring until, yes, it had finally died. But there'd been nothing wrong with the charger.

"Well, why didn't you—" Frank began, but Sky was the one to interrupt this time.

"Hey, where's Poppy? Which field's she in?"

Frank's eyes squinted her way, measuring.

"You remember that Poppy was bred toward the end of the season," he said at last. "So she's over in the east field with all the late-foaling mares."

"Okay, then." Sky leaned in to give Lady Blue some extra love. "I'll be back," she whispered. "I'll be back!" she called to the others. And then she took off running, straight down the fence line.

"Hey, where you think you're going?" Frank yelled after. "You've got stuff to unload and chores to do, girly, don't forget that!"

"I know!" Sky turned without stopping, jogging backward for a bit. "I won't stay long, I promise! But I've got to see Poppy. I've got to say hello!"

Frank was scowling of course, but it was mostly for show.

All bark and barely any bite, that was Frank Massey.

Sky grinned and swung back around, picking up speed as she went. A few of the mares kept pace with her until the next green fence loomed. And then they peeled off and away, whinnying to Sky but circling back to rejoin the herd.

4

Here's the story with Poppy, why she's special:

It was nearly four years before, and Sky was knee-deep in damp straw, rubbing a long-legged filly down like Sky had been doing since she could hold a towel. Rubbing the towel rough because that's what you have to do in order to wipe away all the blood and the damp, the shock of being born.

The filly had been fast coming out, which was typical for her dam, and she was dark-looking to start. But with all the rubbing, she was shining up bright and red, like most Shaughnessy foals will do, bright and red like a new copper penny.

She still had her little slippers on of course. Golden slippers they're called, although really they're whitish gray. A membrane wrapping around the mini-hooves like socks, keeping the mare from getting cut from the inside as the foal is coming through.

The golden slippers were already starting to peel

away—that's what they do right after birth, they peel away and shrivel to nothing—and Sky counted out three perfect white socks, laughing at the missing one.

"Figures," she said, pointing it out to her father. "She was in too much of a hurry to put on the last sock."

"She was in a hurry all right," her father agreed. "We barely made it for her grand entrance."

"But she brought us a flower for our trouble," Sky said, nodding to the white blaze in the middle of her forehead. Not a star exactly—too round and full.

"Looks like some kind of a flower, a small one. . . ." Sky was trying to think of which she meant. Her mother had a book of flowers, common and rare.

"A poppy," her father offered.

"Poppy," she repeated. And then she held the damp head between her hands, angling it gently so she could see into one big brown eye, judge how alert the filly was, and that's when it happened—something passed between them, something clicked.

Her father told her it happens that way with a horse sometimes, same as with people. You fall hard for one out of all the rest in the whole wide world.

Poppy didn't belong to Sky of course. The filly was Shaughnessy-bred, which meant she was currently owned by Archibald Shaughnessy MacIntyre II. Shaughnessy Farms had been in the MacIntyre (or Mac for short) family for over a hundred years.

All Sky and Poppy ever got was about three months out of a whole year. But it never mattered. Once they were together, it was like they'd never been apart.

And so when Sky caught a glimpse of Poppy on the far side of the east field that day, grazing in a string of other mares, she didn't even bother whistling or calling. She just started running—fast as she could, fast as her two legs would go. Which is actually pretty slow compared to what four legs can do. Humans are just plain puny when it comes to running, that's what Sky had always thought.

But it didn't matter how slow she was, not really. Because Poppy had seen Sky and now she was running too, and in no time flat they were together.

"Poppy, Poppy, Poppy."

Sky threw her arms as far as they would go around the horse's great neck, and put her nose right into the pulsing flesh, inhaling deeply. It was everything she loved—horse and wind and grass and hay and sweet feed. And something else, something new.

"You're going to have a foal."

Of course Sky knew it already. But it was the first time she'd seen Poppy since the horse had officially become a mare.

"You're going to make such a good mama, the best," Sky

told her, and then she was—quick—pressing her whole face into Poppy's warm neck. Because just saying the word *mama* had made something start to pop open, and Sky needed to push it down, seal it off fast.

Poppy stayed still but gave a questioning nicker, instantly sensing that something was wrong.

"I missed you is all," Sky whispered, which was true. But not everything, not by a long shot. Sky knew she'd be telling Poppy about her mother soon enough, but she wasn't ready yet.

"I missed you so much," she said again, and then she took a deep breath and started rambling on like she always did when she first got back, catching Poppy up on where they'd been, what they'd been doing.

How they'd gone on from Shaughnessy last year to the September sales in Lexington as usual, how handsome her father had looked as he worked the show, bringing the geldings and mares and stallions out into the auction ring, some of them going for a million dollars each.

Then she was telling about New York. How they'd gone all the way up to Saratoga for the fall racing season to work for some fancy horse friends of the Macs. And then it was back down to Florida to winter like always.

Sky knew she was leaving out a bunch. How they'd stopped at the hospital in New York City, the one they'd been told could work miracles. How they'd stayed there for a while until they realized there were no miracles to work.

Then it was down south again, in and out of the last hospital, the one that said all they could do was give her mother stuff for the pain.

But Sky skipped all that.

"You should've seen the waves!" Sky told her. Because Poppy was always curious about the ocean. "Big as a barn sometimes when it's storming. Alive. The water keeps trying to grab you, push you down."

Poppy had been to plenty of tracks. But she'd never done any racing near the shore. So all she knew was ponds or streams, water that wasn't strong or deep enough to be a threat.

She liked hearing about the silver dolphins gliding through the water, and the raggedy brown pelicans swooping down out of the sky for a fish snack, and the seagulls fighting rowdy and rough over one crust of bread.

"There's not much grass where we go," Sky told her. Because Poppy, like any horse, always liked reports on the quality of grass. "And there aren't any horses down that far, none like you, just some grumpy ponies, poor old things."

Why do you go? Why do you leave?

That's what Poppy was asking, and it was an old question, the same each year.

If Sky loved it here in Kentucky, if she loved Poppy, why did she leave?

And it was always hard for Sky to explain. Because the truth was, leaving Kentucky had never been her wish. Her mother had loved horse country, but she'd loved the ocean more. Which is why they'd always gone south for the winter, all the way down, to the very tip of Florida. A place where they could park their trailer far out in the middle of nowhere.

They'd lie on the beach all day, all night sometimes. Which was fine before, but terrible after her mother was gone.

Because that's when Sky's father started turning ghost. Barely there, even when he was sitting right beside her. Not there at all sometimes. Disappearing for days—nights, even. Scaring Sky half to death. Coming back looking terrible, smelling worse.

Why do you go, then, why do you leave me?

Honestly, she wasn't sure if it was Poppy repeating the question, or if the words were just there, floating around inside her own head. But she had an answer ready anyhow.

"I'm here now," Sky murmured, leaning her whole body into Poppy, all of her weight. "I'm here now. And I'm not going away." She said it louder this time. Maybe because it was exactly what she herself had been wanting to hear.

5

Poppy was a maiden mare, which meant that she'd never foaled before. Most of the mares grouped with Poppy in this east field were maiden.

Juniper. Shaker Rose. Callabee. Circe.

"Hello there," Sky said as each familiar horse pushed their way into the circle, tired of letting Poppy have all the fun.

"Hello, hello, my sweet girls. Hello!"

One by one the mares stepped forward, bumping their soft noses to her chest, shoulders, the top of her head. Breathing in the girl's scent, sending their own hot breath back. A proper greeting.

"How's everybody doing?" Sky asked, and instantly the air sparked with feelings, the ghost of images.

There'd been a fair amount of confusion as to what was going on inside their own bodies—the widening, the thickening, the heaviness. The movement inside their bellies. There'd been some pain.

"No pain now?" Sky quickly asked.

No pain now.

A mostly collective answer.

"Good." She put a palm flat to Shaker Rose's belly. "It'll all be over soon, and you'll have your foals right under your feet all the time, following you everwhere."

The mares cupped their ears at Sky's words, blinked their dark eyes, considering. They were trying to see what was ahead, she could feel it. But it was fuzzy—the notion of the future always fuzzy to a horse. The past was easier; it came in pieces, in waves. Clearer for some horses than others.

Every horse is singular, Sky knew from an early age, every horse is unique. Not so different from people, really. Every horse has its own personality, quirks and tics, strengths and weaknesses.

Poppy's strength was her curiosity, her eagerness to learn—not just about the usual horse things, her job as a racehorse: the rules of the barn, the track, the race itself.

No, Poppy was especially observant, quick to read a situation. But she was patient too, which was a little unusual for a horse so smart—sometimes extremely smart horses could be less tolerant of faults in others, horse or human. But Poppy was patient and calm, wise.

"She's an old soul," Sky's father had said straightaway. Which is probably why they'd clicked.

"Sky's an old soul, I'm sure," Sky's mother always insisted. "She's been around this world a few times, no doubt about that."

Sky's mother had been big into reincarnation. Which means that after you die, you come back as something else. Not just once or twice, but over and over again until you get "it" right.

Sky had never totally been clear on what "it" was. And what happened after that. But of course she didn't mind the idea of somebody coming back after they died. Especially not now.

Her mother had wanted to be a bird—Sky knew exactly what kind, but she didn't want to think about that right now. She needed to tuck it away like so much else.

Run. Run. Run.

The word was buzzing through her brain from the horses, and a sudden breeze was ruffling across the pastures, teasing the herd with a whiff of spring.

Run. Run. Run.

The mares breathed it in. They flicked their tails and tossed their heads. Pranced a step or two.

"Go on!" Sky urged the group. "Don't wait for me! Go!"

And so they did, bursting off and away. Rushing out across the half brown field—all of them together, except for Poppy.

Let's go. Let's run.

That's what Poppy was saying, bobbing her head, poking her nose at Sky, making it clear that she wanted them to go together.

What are you waiting for?

"For Frank to yell at me!" Sky answered Poppy's question out loud.

It was against Shaughnessy rules to ride any of the pregnant mares, though riding a mare as compact as Poppy still was—the foal hadn't yet dropped into place—wouldn't actually hurt anything.

"Don't want to get into trouble my first day here, do I?"

Poppy gave a snort, took a few steps away, then back again.

"Go on!" Sky said, giving her a light slap on the rump. "I don't mind, really. I'd rather be running too! Go on!"

But it was no use. Poppy circled once, then twice. Finally she came to a dead stop right in front of Sky, bowing her head low, her front legs too.

"Oh, Poppy," Sky sighed. "I'm not going to ride you. I'm not!"

Still she glanced back toward the foaling barn, knowing deep down that it was too far off for Frank—for anyone—to see. She turned to scan the fields in all directions, but they were a long way from any barn.

Sky let out another sigh, but she felt herself giving in. The temptation was just too much. "Okay, you win. But just this once."

And then Sky was reaching up, clutching a hunk of Poppy's mane—strong as any rope. Swinging herself up and over, settling in for the ride.

The moment Sky was in place, Poppy wheeled around and shot off across the field, running full out. Sky wound the mane tighter between her fingers and hunkered down for speed.

The rest of the herd was far, far ahead by now. But the distance was like a dare, and in the blink of an eye, Poppy and Sky were just a tail behind, then nothing but a nose.

"Go, Poppy, go," Sky whispered, and in the next breath they were bursting through the tangle of bodies, surging through and past.

Sky felt a sizzle, a zap like lightning, and she knew this was what jockeys felt—what Frank himself must have felt years and years ago—when their horses came from behind, terrible odds, only to win it all.

Poppy was in the lead now, and the rest of the herd fanned

out behind, following in her wake. The ground shook with so much running, so many hooves pounding, so many hearts beating at once. And Sky knew what it was like to be many, not just one.

Together the herd surged over the highs and lows of the field, the places where the land went flat and straight. The world stretched out, forever almost, and there was nothing to stop them, nothing to get in their way.

Except a figure. Rising up from one of the sudden lows, rising up all at once, like a flock of birds startled out of the grass. Only it wasn't birds, it was a person—a boy.

"Go 'round," Sky breathed, but she was too slow, too *human*. The herd had already split in two, streaming past the boy, great red bodies rippling by, water flowing around a rock.

Sky locked eyes with the boy as she went flying by. The boy's eyes were bright, startled wide—blue maybe, or gray.

Gone again, just like that. The stream rushing back together, the herd thundering on.

Sky ducked her head beneath her arm, tucking it under to glance back behind her, the way jockeys do to check their position on the track without losing any speed.

The boy had turned as well. He was watching Sky, not with the naked eye but, strangely, with a pair of binoculars poised in place.

Who are you?

That's what Sky wondered, but she couldn't stop to ask. The mares had reached a dizzying speed, and Sky hunkered down again, held on tight.

It was a weightless feeling—moving so fast, nearly flying. She knew why her mother had wanted to be a bird, the whole world rushing past, a swirl of brown and green and blue. She wished it could stay like this, a blur, forever. But she knew it couldn't.

"Whoa," she murmured low in her throat when she saw the green fencing rising up in the distance, the end of Shaughnessy land. "Whoa," she said again, though it wasn't necessary at all.

The herd had already started slowing as one in order to make the wide turn together, swooping and dipping, swallows moving in flight. Circling back across the field, back the way they'd so quickly traveled.

Sky sat up tall on Poppy's bare back as they slowed to a satisfied gallop. She squinted through the glare of sun, but there was nothing to see. The herd was coming to the hollowed-out place they'd passed before, but the spot was empty, the boy was gone.

6

Most farms the Dorans worked, they stayed in their trailer or they bunked down in some empty back room. Shaughnessy was different. Here they had their very own apartment, the Doran Suite, the Macs had named it years before, in James's honor.

The Doran Suite was at the back of the foaling barn, same as with a lot of farms, but it was a true apartment with a kitchen and two bedrooms plus a bathroom that boasted a tub, not just a shower.

"Our vacation home," Sky's mother had always called it, even though they'd never been vacationing at Shaughnessy, always working. But the Shaughnessy barns were so fancy, inside and out, that the Doran Suite was nicer even than any hotel they'd ever been to.

Once Sky got back from her secret ride on Poppy, it

took a while to get settled. Besides the usual unloading, old friends kept stopping by to say their hellos—the farmhands, Tex and Skeet; the main grooms, Cesar, Victor, and Ross; the assistant manager, Wick.

Everybody started off by exclaiming over how tall Sky was, how much she'd grown, as if that was the main change. Then there'd be that terrible pause, the tears welling up, the word *sorry* repeated over and over again.

So sorry.

"Thanks."

That's what Sky kept answering back. Even though it sounded wrong. Saying thanks for the very worst thing in the world happening.

The barn cats and farm dogs were a whole lot easier. When Sky dropped down to the ground for a first greeting, it was just plain purring and tail-wagging happiness at seeing her again. No sadness, no tears, none whatsoever. No words.

Two of her longtime favorite barn cats, Gray and Lucy, stalked Sky to the Doran Suite and stayed while she got her room settled. Sky was determined to make the bed and put her clothes away straight off, same as her mother always did. And she intended to do the same for her father because she knew he would never take the time.

But she stopped cold at the doorway to his room, unable

to go inside. Through the open door she could see her father's two khaki duffles on the floor where he'd flung them. She could see his extra pairs of work boots lying in a pile. But there was nothing of her mother's in there, nothing at all. They'd left her things in the trailer parked at the back of the farm, and the total absence made it nearly impossible to go on in.

Sky was about to give up, turn around, when something whizzed past her ankle. Two somethings—fast and furry.

It was Gray and Lucy, both of them dashing across the floor and taking a flying leap onto the big bare mattress, tumbling over each other.

They tussled, rolled, and then all at once the cats stopped, just like that. They perched on the mattress, alert and still. Heads cocked like they were listening to something far off. But they were watching Sky, big yellow eyes hardly blinking at all.

Sky couldn't speak cat of course.

"We're not Dr. Dolittles or something," her father had told her once when she'd asked why they could only talk to horses.

But Sky knew what the cats were telling her.

Come on in! Get it over with! You'll feel better that way.

So she took one step into the room, then another. She

stopped and breathed it in. Cedar and a hint of mothballs. Nothing flowery, not a bit of the gardenia lotion her mother had always used.

Sky had the urge to bolt, just like a spooked horse. But the cats pinned her with their yellow eyes—powerful and strange. And that kept her going. Step by step. All the way across the room. She made it to the cedar chest, was able to take out the sheets and quilt, the pillowcases.

Later she would swear that Lucy and Gray helped her make up the bed—batting at the sheets, rolling from one end to the other.

When it was finally done, everything ready in her father's room, she sat for a moment and the cats rubbed up against her on either side, furry bookends, purring like mini furnaces.

"Thanks," Sky murmured, truly meaning it, and the cats blinked up at her—once, twice—and then they were gone, a blur of motion, darting straight through the door, out into the rest of the barn.

7

*B*andages, bandage scissors, shoulder-length latex gloves, baler's twine, thermometers, saline solution, sterilized syringes, garbage bags, washcloths, towels, cotton bedsheets, halters, lead ropes, buckets, flashlights, and extra batteries.

After Sky and her father were done with their first inventory of the supply room, they scouted around out back to check on how many bales of hay and alfalfa Frank had had delivered.

"Plenty for the first week," her father said. "But we're low on bags of sweet feed and cans of molasses."

Sky wrote it all down on one sheet, then started a separate grocery list for the two of them.

Peanut butter, jelly, bread, milk, orange juice, coffee, chocolate bars (for energy), cans of Dr Pepper (because it was her father's favorite), microwave popcorn, microwave dinners.

Soon enough they'd be "in the weeds," as Frank called it, crazy busy. Because once the mares really started foaling, Sky and her father would never be sitting down to a proper meal. They'd always be grabbing whatever they could eat on the go and drinking tons of coffee to keep them awake during the night, when mares are most likely to foal.

Her father liked his coffee strong and black, but Sky liked hers milky sweet. So she added sugar to the list, and then she added oatmeal cookies and peppermints, thinking of all the mares she knew with a sweet tooth, including Poppy of course.

After that was finished, Sky's father thrust something toward her—the leather-bound journal with all the mares listed alongside their approximate due dates.

"You can handle this, yeah?" he said.

Sky froze. It was her mother's job—typing up all the information from the handwritten pages, making a spreadsheet. Her father was hopeless with computers.

"Yeah, I think so." She took the book and held it to her chest, glancing up.

A looker.

That's what her mother had always said about her father.

A charmer, too.

But James Doran had been rode hard and put up wet, as the horse saying goes—especially clear to Sky now that they'd returned to a world so tidy and neat. His jet-black hair was streaked with gray—when had that happened? It fell, unkempt, nearly to his shoulders. He hadn't shaved in weeks, and his beard had new bits of gray in it as well. His eyes were bloodshot, the way they mostly were lately. From crying so much—that's what she told herself.

"I can do it, Dad," Sky said, firmly now, and he reached out and put a hand on her shoulder.

"Good girl." He pulled her close for a moment, kissed her forehead. "What would I do without you?" he murmured before moving off. Sky felt her eyes pricking, but she blinked a few times.

Be strong.

That's what she told herself as she headed to the desk, flipped on the computer. She let the office chair spin a few times as the program loaded.

The office was at the center of the foaling barn, like a heart. One whole wall was made up of clear Plexiglas so you could see right into a few of the stalls without going out the door into the main aisle.

Every stall was empty now, spotless—cleaned and sterilized by somebody else since the Dorans hadn't been there early enough to do it—but this time tomorrow the whole place would be buzzing with horse life. And Sky couldn't wait.

There was nothing better, in Sky's opinion, than a barn full of horses. Sky loved the regular sounds—the snorting and snuffling, the chomping of hay and stomping of hooves. She loved the not-so-regular sounds too, the ones only she and her father could hear—the jumbled-up thoughts and feelings, the pieces of dreams she'd catch as she'd be coming into the barn while the mares were still dozing. Sky couldn't wait till tomorrow for all that to fill up her head, her time, so nothing else could.

In the meantime, she pulled her chair closer to the desk and clicked on the spreadsheet icon, flexed her fingers, and started typing. She'd be putting in all fifty-two mares' names—and not just the first names or the nicknames but the full official, registered names.

Usually a horse's official name had something to do with the dam (the mom) and the sire (the dad). For instance, Poppy's full name was Poppy Fields Forever. The Poppy part came from that blaze between her eyes. But the Fields came from her dam, Fields on Fire, and the Forever was from her sire, Forever Takes Time.

Once Sky was done with the names, she went on to add all the individual information, like whether the mare had foaled before and if so, how many times. Whether or not she'd had any injuries, maybe from racing or from showing. If she needed any particular medicine or vitamins or special food.

Of course her father kept everything filed away inside his head. He didn't need the leather-bound book or the spread-sheets. His memory was perfect when it came to his mares—and Sky was nearly the same.

Still, it was important to have every piece of information organized and updated so there wouldn't be any mistakes. Because it wasn't just Sky and her father looking after the Shaughnessy mares, although they were in charge during foaling. There'd be a whole string of people coming and going—a couple of night watchmen plus a few interns, residents from the local animal hospital studying to be vets.

"Done with that yet?"

Frank's voice, startling her from behind. She thought he'd gone back to the main barn.

"Nah, not yet."

"Slow going, then?"

"Not bad. Just takes time, you know."

Frank came close, peered over her shoulder.

"Where'd you learn to do that anyway? Computers? Charts? They teach you that in school?" He gave it a beat, then snapped his fingers. "Oh, that's right, you don't go to school."

"I go to school!" It was an old jab Frank always used to get her riled up, and it never failed. "Lots of people homeschool now," she mumbled. "It's not that big a deal."

"In my day, we'd call 'home school' playing hooky."

"It's not playing hooky! I learn as much as any other kid who sits at a desk all day, more probably. Like computers, for instance. I know a lot. A whole lot more than you, *old man*."

"Hey!" Frank poked at her arm. "You're becoming a real chip off the old block, so watch it." He plopped down into the chair near the desk, the worn leather La-Z-Boy that had been in the same place for as long as Sky could remember. As soon as Frank was settled, Burley was right at his feet, brown eyes pleading to be picked up.

"And this old thing here—spoiled rotten, that's what *he* is," Frank tutted, but he was already bending down to gently heft the fat little body into his lap, settling him just so.

Sky went back to working on the log, and Frank rambled on for a while about the weather, the mild winter, the lack of snow.

"Now all that homeschooling stuff," Frank backtracked, "your mother, God rest her soul"—crossing himself—"she kept on top of that, didn't she?"

Sky nodded, eyes glued to the screen. "Yeah, she did."

"Your dad, he helping you with that now?"

Sky hesitated, but just for a beat. "Yeah," she told him. It was a lie, and she wasn't sure exactly what made her say it. But there it was.

"And you're doing the work?" Frank asked.

"Yeah." Lie number two.

The truth was, her mother had left a whole year of lesson plans, all of them separated into folders and labeled, she was that organized. But Sky hadn't been able to open them—not one. She couldn't look at all those pages yet, her mother's beautiful tiny script everywhere.

"What about—" Frank started, and Sky wasn't sure she could handle three lies in a row, knew she couldn't handle talking so much about her mother, so she blurted out the thing that had been bothering her since her secret ride with Poppy.

"Is somebody visiting the Macs? One of the grandkids?"

Now that Sky'd had time to think, she knew who the boy standing in the field was, but she wanted Frank to confirm it.

"Oh, that's right, meant to tell you. Archie's here. The youngest grandson."

Sky nodded. "Archibald Shaughnessy MacIntyre, the fourth," she intoned, the whole thing—so formal!

"It's a mouthful, that's for sure," Frank acknowledged.

"They here on vacation?" Sky asked. It was unusual for

this side of the Mac clan to visit during foaling season. The parents lived in Washington, DC, but both traveled all over the world for work—something important, international, United Nations maybe. Sky had actually only met Archie a couple of times in all the years she'd been coming to Shaughnessy.

"The boy's here on his own," Frank said. "His parents had to go to Uganda for a few months. Not sure if it's a permanent assignment. So they wanted him to stay here, finish out the school year in the United States and then they'll see."

Sky chewed at the tender inside of her cheek. Archie had probably already told his grandparents what he'd seen—Sky riding Poppy. The Macs were almost like family, but they were still the bosses. They would not be happy with her.

"Maybe it'll be good to have him here," Frank was saying. "Somebody your own age around for a change. Or just about. A year older, I think."

Sky gave him a look. "Why do I need someone my own age around here?" she asked. Sometimes there were other kids at the farms they worked; sometimes she was the only one. It had never mattered much.

"Because . . . ," Frank began, but then he let the sentence

drift. Sky had a feeling he was going to tie the answer some-how to her mother.

"Doesn't matter to me," she blurted, giving an exagger-ated shrug. "I like hanging out with old farts like you."

"I'm not too old to show you a thing or two!" He poked at her again. "And never forget it."

"Okay, okay!" she cried. "Can I get back to work now?"

"Who's stopping you?"

Sky opened her mouth, closed it again. Went back to typing. Frank stayed quiet too, and after a short while his breathing slowed and a soft rattling started up—both man and dog had nodded off.

Sky got lost in the work again, making sure all the infor-mation got transferred from book to computer. Time passed, and she was nearly finished when something flashed in front of her face.

Frank's hand. He was awake now, and he was hold-ing something out to her—a piece of striped peppermint. Offering it like she was a horse.

Sky gave a snort because of course she didn't mind. Most times she'd rather be a horse.

The day her mother died, she'd started running down the beach, fast as her legs would go. She'd wanted to keep run-ning, miles and miles and miles and miles. And if she'd been a horse, she could have.

"Neigh."

That's what Sky replied, totally deadpan. And it made Frank laugh like she knew it would.

The old man handed over the peppermint, then reached into his pocket for another. At first he made like he was giving her a second piece. But then he pulled his hand back just as Sky was reaching for it, and popped the mint into his own mouth, still laughing.

8

On a horse farm, your day pretty much begins halfway through your night. Which was fine by Sky, especially that foaling season.

Idle hands are the devil's playthings—that's what Frank always said. And even though Sky didn't really believe in the devil, she'd come to understand over the past few months the meaning behind the words.

Some people need to be busy or the world goes off. James Doran was one of those people; Sky was another.

So on that first real morning back, she was thankful to have a reason to be up and dressed long before the sun could even think about rising, thankful her father had a reason too.

First off they loaded the wheelbarrows full of new straw and went from stall to stall, unloading it and making comfy beds for the twenty-five mares coming in later that morning.

Once that was done, they set out the hay nets and water buckets. Then they sorted through the brass nameplates, sliding them into their slots beside each stall door, choosing the order carefully, since mares in foal are picky about their neighbors.

Sky and her father paused halfway through the chores to drink some coffee, to watch the sunrise—their first back in Kentucky.

One layer of bright purple seeping through the black morning sky, and then streaks of orange and pink on top of that, shimmers of golden yellow in between like layer cake frosting.

"Wow, she's a doozy," Sky whispered. Careful not to talk too loud and break the spell. Careful not to say "master-piece," her mother's word for a particularly lovely sunrise, which had been her favorite time of day.

A new beginning.

That's what Sky's mother used to call it.

A fresh start—every single day. A moment of grace.

"Grace," Sky said, her voice still barely there. Her father reached for her hand, held it tight, then let it go.

"Better get back to work," he said.

By the time Frank appeared, two hours later, with a Tupperware bowl of the spaghetti he'd made them special the night before—Sky's favorite dish—the barn was ready for the mares.

"You two've been busy!" Frank cried, scanning the aisles.

"What'd you expect, old man?" her father tossed back.

"Nothing less, nothing less."

Sky gobbled the spaghetti down cold, not bothering with the microwave. It was even better left over, in her opinion. She offered some to her father, but he wrinkled his nose and stuck with his coffee.

For the rest of the morning it was a clamor of hooves and horse thoughts as the Dorans started transferring the first twenty-five mares, the ones with the earliest due dates, getting them settled into the foaling barn.

Old hands like Lady Blue, Darsha, and Miss Lynn took to their new digs like it was no big deal, but some of the maiden mares were sensitive about being moved from the barns they were used to.

Marigold and Dulcimer in particular got all riled up, kicking and stomping, noisy with complaints.

"Come on now, ladies," Sky's father softly murmured. "Nothing to be scared of. We want you to be more comfortable, that's all. Take a look at that nice soft straw you've got to lay your head on, and that lovely cold water. We'll be bringing you a snack in no time flat. Treating you like queens, that's what we're fixing to do."

Dulcimer, always a bit of a diva, pricked her ears at what was being said. She had a notion, Sky knew, of what kind of treatment a queen might get, and she was all for it. She pranced about her stall, nosing at the fresh straw, checking the thickness, finally content.

"Hey there, luv, you know all this commotion's bad for your foal," her father was telling Marigold next.

Sky could hear the mare considering, thinking better of rearing up, and that's when the Macs appeared.

"She's not giving you any trouble, is she, James?" Mr. Mac's deep voice echoed through the barn.

"Not a bit of it, sir," her father called back, settling Marigold in the next instant, sliding her into the stall, easy as pie. "Not a bit."

Mrs. Mac was a champion hugger, and she had Sky in a tight hold before she knew it.

"Oh, Sky, I'm so very sorry," Mrs. Mac was saying, close to her ear. "So very sorry about your mother. If there's anything we can do, anything at all . . ." Her voice broke, and Sky's own throat closed up the way it did when somebody else started crying.

"Thanks," Sky managed—that stupid word—before being gently pushed on to Mr. Mac.

"Why, just look at this long-legged filly!" Mr. Mac hugged

her, then held her at arm's length. "Getting nearly as tall as you, Slim!"

Slim was Mrs. Mac's nickname from when she'd been a model long ago—tall and slim and gorgeous. And in Sky's opinion she hadn't changed much over the years. Her face was lined of course, and her long smooth hair had gone completely silver, but she was still beautiful. And she always looked like she'd just stepped out of the pages of some fashion magazine, even when she was just hanging around the barn.

"Taller than Archie, will you look at that?" Mr. Mac stepped back, and there he was, the boy from the field.

"Sky, you remember Archie, don't you?" Mrs. Mac asked. "I know it's been a while."

Sky nodded to Archie, but she couldn't quite look him in the eye. She wondered if he'd already told on her. The Macs weren't acting angry, but maybe they were just waiting for the right moment to scold her.

"Actually, we saw each other yesterday," Archie said, and that's when their eyes met and locked, the way they had in the field.

"You did?" Mrs. Mac cried.

"I was—" Sky knew it was best to come clean herself. "I was—" But Archie cut her off.

"She was busy with some of the horses. I just said a quick

hello and moved on. Didn't want to get in the way." Archie glanced at the floor.

Sky opened her mouth. She could still tell about riding Poppy, *should* tell.

"You might have given the girl a hand, Archie!" Mr. Mac said, his big, jolly voice turning the tiniest bit sharp. "A boy should spend all the time he can outside in the fresh air, *doing* something, not just . . ." Mr. Mac gestured in the air. "Holed up in his room."

There was a moment of awkward silence, but then Frank filled it.

"Ah, well, plenty of time for that!" he said, slapping Archie on the back, pushing him on down the aisle. "Let's take a look at the mares, shall we? Isn't that what you're here for?"

"Yes, yes, of course." Mrs. Mac laughed.

They went from stall to stall, and Sky could feel all the tension from the move melting away. One by one the mares came to the gate, and the Macs paused for a murmur and a pat, a kiss on the nose.

The Macs were good owners—the best. Horses loved it here. Occasionally the Dorans had worked places where the horses weren't happy, and if Sky's father couldn't do something about it, if the owners wouldn't let him, they would leave.

"So, James, who do you think will go first, which mare?" Mr. Mac asked halfway through the tour. It was the same question he always posed at the start of foaling.

And Sky's father gave his usual evasive answer. "Ah now, Mr. Mac, you know I can't say for sure." It was definitely bad luck to make any predictions out loud.

"But I gather a few are bagging up, isn't that so?" Mr. Mac persisted, like he always did.

"Yessir," James answered. "Lady Blue of course, and Darsha. Floss, too."

"'Bagging up' means that the mare's milk is starting to fill her udders," Mrs. Mac explained to Archie. "It's usually a sign that there'll be a foal soon."

"But it's not always reliable," Frank threw in. "You see, son, sometimes a mare will bag up for weeks and the foal will be late. And sometimes a mare will be flat as a pancake and you'll get a surprise in the middle of the night."

"Isn't there a way to tell, a real way?" Archie asked, and Sky noticed how his voice was different from the Macs, different from her own. Clipped, formal-sounding. Nothing soft or rounded. "Isn't there an X-ray?" he continued. "Or an ultrasound like they do for women when they're pregnant?"

"You can call a vet, sure," Frank answered. "If there's trouble. But there's never any trouble here."

"Not with the Dorans around!" Mr. Mac grinned at James. "Isn't that right?"

"Yessir, you bet," Sky's father returned the grin and gave a wink, too—a flash of the old charm and confidence.

But as soon as the Macs had moved off, the sureness fell away and Sky watched her father tuck a hand quickly into the V of his shirt, reaching for the St. Christopher medal. The familiar gesture made her own fingers itch for a good-luck charm, a new one to replace what her mother had given her, what she'd broken, months ago. But there was nothing, so she did the only thing she could think to do: rap her knuckles three times against the green wood trimming on the nearest stall door.

Old-school luck, knocking on wood. But good for now—better than good. The Shaughnessy green was flush with luck, everybody knew that. And it surrounded the whole place like a lucky green force field. Nothing could touch them here.

When Sky looked up, she saw that everyone had moved on to the next aisle—everyone except Archie. He had drifted off to one of the open side doors. She hesitated, but just for a moment.

"Thanks for not telling about riding Poppy," she said, her voice low, when she came up beside him. "It wouldn't hurt her—I'd never hurt a horse. But it's against the rules here, to ride a mare when she's in foal."

"Oh." Archie gave a quick sideways glance. "That's not why—"

"Well, thanks just the same," Sky said, wanting to have it done, over. She didn't like to feel beholden to anyone.

"Sure." Archie glanced at her again, then leaned down to look at something. A couple of black-and-gold caterpillars inching toward his shoe.

"Those are tent worms," Sky told him, thinking he must not have seen them before. "Or tent caterpillars they're called too. Because they spin these webs in tree branches that sort of look like tents."

Archie cleared his throat. "Actually, it's the eastern tent caterpillar. *Malacosoma americanum.*"

"Okay." Sky let out a laugh. "I guess you don't need me to tell you about them."

"We have them at home," Archie explained. "But usually they come much later in the spring."

"I guess you're right," Sky agreed, thinking about it. "Closer to April. When it's warmer."

"But it's been a mild winter. Not very cold. Hardly any snow," he said, more to himself. Then he reached out and plucked up one and then the other—gently, almost tenderly—so they were both cradled in his palm.

"They're more prickly than you would think," he said, standing and turning to her, holding his hand out.

Automatically she took a step back. "That's okay."

"Are you afraid of bugs?" He seemed surprised.

"No." She wasn't scared of bugs, but she wasn't crazy about them either. For some reason, though, she felt like she had to prove herself. "It *is* prickly," she admitted after running a finger lightly down one tiny body. "Like a mini bristle brush."

"A mini bristle brush," Archie repeated. "Hmmm."

"And those look like eyes." She pointed to the gold spots going straight down both backs. "Yellow eyes."

"Yes, that's what they're meant to look like." Archie nodded. "To scare bigger bugs and birds away. To keep from being eaten. Camouflage, too."

Sky swiped her hand down the back of her jeans. No real reason—the caterpillar wasn't wet or slimy—but she couldn't help it. "I guess I thought they'd feel softer, like woolly worms, you know, the ones that come in the fall?"

"*Pyrrharctia isabella,*" Archie said. "Woolly worms."

Sky gave him a look. "Do you know the scientific name for every kind of caterpillar?"

"Pretty much. I know the scientific name for most bugs."

"Wow." Sky wasn't sure what else to say. "*Equus ferus*

caballus," she blurted finally, remembering. "The scientific name for horse."

"Right!" Archie's eyes lit up. Definitely gray, not blue. A smooth, even gray, the color of slate. And there was a pale splash of freckles across the bridge of his nose.

"Did you know that woolly worms can predict the weather?" she said then, suddenly remembering something else, something her mother had told her when she was little. "They can predict how bad the winter's going to be."

Archie gave a small shake of his head, so Sky continued. "You check the brown band around the middle. If the band's thick, it'll be a mild winter. But if it's thin, so that the woolly worm is mostly black, the winter's going to be long and cold. Lots of ice and snow."

Archie shook his head, firmly this time. "Actually, that's not true." His eyes swept down to the wriggling caterpillars in his palm. "It's something people used to believe in when they didn't know any better."

"What do you mean, 'didn't know any better'?"

Archie's eyes focused on her again. "I mean, it's like an old wives' tale or something, a myth. It's not real. It's not scientific."

"I don't think something has to be scientific to be real." Sky felt her face heating up, her whole body heating up, though she wasn't sure why exactly.

"You can't prove it," Archie continued, saying the words slowly, carefully, like he was speaking to a small child, a not-very-bright small child. Looking at her that way too. "Caterpillars predicting weather. It's not something you can actually prove."

"You can prove it," Sky heard herself saying even as a little voice inside her head was asking, *Can you prove it?* She thought of her mother's hand, her mother's finger smoothing down a woolly worm's black-and-brown fluff. She felt hot all over, and she knew her cheeks were completely pink now, which was ridiculous. Why did people blush anyway? Horses didn't blush.

"It *is* true," Sky added quietly, and then she turned and headed off to catch up with her father and Frank and the Macs. It was silly to be standing around talking about bugs when there were horses to see to.

9

A mare will usually foal at night. The instinct goes deep down, all the way to the very core of what a horse is: a prey animal.

Hard to believe that something as mighty as a horse is vulnerable enough to be prey—what with their big, strong bodies, their muscular legs, hard hooves, powerful jaws and teeth. But in the animal kingdom, if you're not a predator, you're prey, and so it is for the horse.

Night acts like a cover, a curtain for prey animals. A mare instinctively knows she can hide in the dark at her weakest moment—when she's foaling. She also knows that by the time the sun rises, her foal will be on its feet, ready to run from danger if it has to.

Of course at Shaughnessy there were no predators—no wild dogs or wolves, a few coyotes maybe, but never enough to be a threat. And anyway, all the mares were kept inside fancy barns, not off in the wild somewhere.

But none of that mattered, Sky had learned early on. Eight out of ten mares will foal in the middle of the night, right when you're sleeping your deepest. And no amount of asking a horse—even if you *can* speak their language—to hold off till a more convenient hour will change their minds.

Some big broodmare farms have high-tech cameras in all the stalls, or fancy sensors, triggered alarms to wake you up if a mare lies down or if her water breaks. Shaughnessy was old-fashioned, though. They still kept a night watchman on guard from sundown to sunrise to keep watch.

"We should change it to 'night watchwoman,'" Sky had said to Gaby when she first met her, years before, after she'd replaced old Ed who'd been at Shaughnessy forever.

"You're right," Gaby had laughed. "But really it's just a name, hon. A title. 'Night watchwoman' is kind of a mouthful anyhow."

From the start, Gaby and Sky's mother had hit it off, and over time they'd gotten close. Gaby moved from job to job on the horse circuit, same as the Dorans did. Working the different sales at different parts of the year, working with different tracks and trainers, broodmare farms.

Sometimes they'd ended up traveling together to a new

job. Lots of times Gaby would come down to visit where they were staying for the winter, before flying off somewhere much more exotic, names Sky would have to look up on a map: the Galápagos Islands or Bali.

Gaby was always looking for adventure, always looking for true love. She liked to tease Maggie, Sky's mother, about finding love so easily—it had walked right up to her own daddy's horse farm in the form of a young James Doran asking for work.

"But the rest of us don't have it handed to us," Gaby would say. "Look at me! I have to go to every far corner of the earth, and I still haven't found it."

"Maybe you're looking too hard," Maggie would tell her.

"Maybe so," Gaby would sigh, but then her expression would turn sly. "It's not all bad, though! I have a little fun now and then."

Which was what Maggie liked to call "an understatement."

Frank called Gaby "wild girl" and almost didn't hire her back one year when she was late getting in from one of her far-off trips. But Sky's mother had persuaded him.

This was Gaby's first night at Shaughnessy for the new season, and as much as Sky wanted to see her, she was dreading the first hello. She was sure Gaby would burst into tears the moment she laid eyes on her, and Sky wasn't sure she could take it.

Crying was not how Gaby handled it, though, not at all. Right away when Sky came into the office that evening, Gaby started talking about her new money venture, showing off the little wooden horses she was carving for the gift shop over at Shakertown.

"I can do about six an hour," Gaby said, lining the wooden horses—each one nearly identical—in a row on the desk. "Not bad. Means I can make an extra buck or two while I'm sitting here all night long waiting on these precious mares to decide to grace us with a foal already."

Sky took up one of the figures, rubbed her thumb down the sloped neck, the smooth-as-silk body. Gaby was always doing something on the side, some little artsy project to make extra money. It always had something to do with horses.

One year she'd made bracelets woven out of horse hair she'd collected from the Shaughnessy mares. One year she bought a bunch of tiny silver horse charms wholesale and strung up earrings and necklaces to sell.

Gaby always got Sky to help with her projects, but she was better at some things than others. Braiding horse hair was easy; making earrings didn't go so well.

"Have you ever done any whittling, hon?" Gaby asked, and when Sky shook her head, Gaby got all excited. "I'll teach you, then! I got an extra knife just for you. And I've got all these blocks of wood a friend of mine gave me from his farm. They're soft maple—real easy to carve into. I bet you'll get the hang of it in no time."

And Gaby was right. After Sky had helped feed and water all the mares for the night, taken their temperatures, and input the new information into the computer log, they settled in beside each other at the desk. Gaby handed Sky a block of wood and a small knife that fit easily in her fingers. She told her not to think about making anything specific yet.

"Just start shaving the knife along the edges," she said. "Let the wood tell you what it wants to be."

It sounded silly but Sky didn't laugh. Because it did seem like the wood had an opinion on how it wanted the knife to go, and Sky tried to follow that.

"Hey, that's pretty good!" Gaby said when she glanced up from her work.

Sky held it out for better inspection, and sure enough, it did already look like something was emerging—a horse, naturally. Just the head for now. Sloped nose, curving jaw-line, a triangle of ear.

"Wow, you're a natural, honey-pie!" Gaby cried. "I knew you would be!"

And she leaned in close to hug Sky with her one free arm, and the hug was about more than just doing her first-ever wood carving. The hug was about Sky's mother, and it was sad but it was good too, and they went back to whittling without completely breaking down in tears.

10

nothing happened that night or the next—no foals jolt-
ing the Dorans out of bed in the wee hours. So Sky and
her father went about their daily chores. Turning out the
mares in the morning, bringing them all back in at night.
Cleaning the stalls while they were empty. Mucking the
manure, scouring the water buckets, forking in the clean new
straw, fluffing up the beds. And when the mares were back
inside their stalls: feeding and watering, wrapping legs, massaging aching muscles. Checking temperatures. Putting any
changes down in the log.

Sky couldn't wait for the first foal to come, but she was
glad to have more time with Poppy before everything got
crazy. After the main chores were through, she could do
whatever she pleased for a couple of hours, and whatever she
pleased usually amounted to roaming the fields with Poppy.

Sky wouldn't ride her again—she told her that straight off. But lots of times they'd play tag, girl and horse, darting back and forth across the pasture.

Of course Poppy always won.

"It's not fair!" Sky cried in a pretend huff. "Two legs against four. Not much of a contest!" She turned away from Poppy, and that's when she caught a glimpse of Archie. He was standing across the field near a row of pines.

"What's he doing?" Sky swung back to the mare, pretending she hadn't seen. "I think he's spying on me." She'd definitely spotted binoculars in that quick look, which was kind of weird. How long had he been there? How long had he been watching? *Why* was he watching?

"Come on, girl, let's go." She gave Poppy's halter a tug. She knew she couldn't avoid Archie forever, even on an eight-hundred-acre farm. But it flashed into her head, the way he'd spoken to her in the foaling barn, the way he'd looked at her—like she was a small child. The way she'd blushed and rushed off—like she really *was* a small child. When she thought of it now, she knew she'd probably overreacted, and it was pretty embarrassing.

"Let's get out of here, girl," Sky mumbled, tugging again. But Poppy had other ideas. She'd caught a whiff of the stranger, and she was curious.

"It's just Archie," Sky told her. "Remember, he's the one we rode by the other day? I told you about him. He's a Mac, but he's . . ." She wasn't sure how to finish the sentence, how to describe him. She wasn't sure what she really thought of him. One minute he seemed nice; the next minute he seemed kind of like a know-it-all.

"Hello, there!"

It was too late now. Archie was calling to her from across the field. "Hello!"

Sky let out a sigh, turned. "Oh, hey!" She waved, acting surprised. "I didn't see you over there." Of course this time when she pulled at Poppy's halter, the mare followed right away.

"I've been out here looking for more caterpillars," Archie explained when Sky was only a few yards away. "Like the ones we saw the other day."

"Are they flying now?" Sky asked. She couldn't help it. She wanted to make sure he understood that she'd seen him watching her through the binoculars.

Archie didn't get it at first, and then he did. His eyes went wide, and one hand clutched at the binoculars, which were resting from a strap around his neck.

"I wasn't. . . I didn't. . . I mean. . ." He kept starting over.

"I'm not going to ride Poppy again." Sky cut to the point.

Why else would he be spying on her? "If that's what you're worried about. I only rode her that one time, and like I said before, it didn't hurt her."

"I know—" Archie began, but Sky cut him off.

"I'd never do anything to hurt Poppy. I'd never hurt any horse. Ever."

"I understand. I believe you."

Sky opened her mouth to keep arguing, but realized she didn't need to.

"Good," she said, and then again, "good," just to be certain.

There was a pause. Sky wasn't sure what to say next, and Archie didn't seem to know either. But then Poppy was nudging her forward.

Let's get on with it, basically was what the mare was saying.

"Okay, okay," Sky grumbled beneath her breath, but then to Archie she said, "This is Poppy. Poppy Fields Forever."

The mare stepped around her, went toward Archie. Sky waited for him to back off. Most people would be intimidated by a great big Thoroughbred coming straight at them, even at a walk.

But Archie stood his ground. He held out the back of one hand, slowly, gently, just like he was supposed to do, so that Poppy could get a good whiff without being startled.

Then he let the hand drift softly along the mare's muzzle, and Poppy let out a low nicker.

"She likes you," Sky said, more than a little surprised. It wasn't like Poppy was a standoffish horse by any means. She was always friendly. But this was different; this was more. Sky could tell Poppy trusted Archie right away, trusted him completely, and that was a big deal. Poppy was usually spot-on when it came to judging people.

"I like her, too," Archie said then, laughing when the mare put her nose to the top of his head, lightly blowing through her nostrils, messing his hair. "Hey, that tickles!"

Sky laughed in spite of herself. "I thought you'd be afraid of horses," she said.

"Why?" Archie seemed genuinely puzzled.

"I don't know," she admitted. "I guess you didn't seem so interested in the foaling barn. And when people aren't interested in horses, it usually means they're afraid." She paused. "Plus you looked really scared that day in the field when I went riding past."

"I *was* scared!" Archie cried. "I thought I was going to be trampled to death by a stampede of horses!"

"They weren't going to *trample* you," Sky scoffed, coming closer, putting a hand to Poppy's rump, moving on to her middle, her shoulder. "They knew you were there before I did."

"Really?" Archie turned his face to her. She was close enough to see the freckles again. "How do you know?"

Sky shrugged, glanced at her fingers spread wide across Poppy's fine red coat. The question felt charged somehow. "You're not dead, are you?"

That made him smile—the Mac smile—one side higher than the other. Maybe she *had* overreacted before, in the barn. Fight or flight. That's the way a horse was wired. Her mother had always said that's the way she was wired too. What did it matter if Archie didn't think woolly worms could predict the weather? She knew it to be true.

"Hey, why do you need those binoculars anyway?" She nodded to his chest. "I mean, I get it if you're watching butterflies, but caterpillars?"

"Well, these are special binoculars." He held them up. "They have both a macro and a micro setting, so I can look at flying insects, but I can also use them on nonflying bugs, use them almost like a microscope. Want to see?"

"Sure," Sky said. Poppy was losing interest in them anyway, getting a whiff of something new—a patch of tender new grass that smelled particularly yummy a few feet away. Might as well let her graze for a bit.

"Here you go." Archie ducked out of the binoculars and handed them over.

They were small and light in Sky's hand. Similar to expensive track glasses, the kind owners like the Macs kept in their pockets or purses—compact but powerful—pulling them out once a race had started to check the position of their horse on the turf.

Sky slipped the strap around her neck, put the scopes to her eye. The pine trees loomed in front of her, blurred, but immediate.

"Wow, these are strong!"

One knob transformed everything in her vision into a green blob, but another knob brought each tiny green pine needle into sharp focus.

"Whoa." She turned slowly to the left, scanning past the pines. She could see the top of Poppy's barn, the tall green cupolas pointing up to the clouds. "Cool." She made a full circle, back to the pines, then gave the binoculars to Archie again.

"Well, I think so, but then I tend to geek out about things like this." Archie gave a quick grimace. He ducked his head, put the strap in place. "Anyway, like I said before, I was looking for caterpillars, and I found a whole bunch over there." He nodded to the trees. "Want to see?"

Sky started to say no. She'd been noticing more and more black-and-gold bodies every day, especially just outside the barn in the afternoons when the blacktop got hot from the sun. She wasn't chomping at the bit to see "a whole bunch." But Archie's eyes were so bright, he seemed so excited to show her. Plus Poppy was still focused on her little patch of heaven.

"Sure," Sky said with a shrug. "Lead the way."

11

*A*t first glance, it was a black rag lying crumpled on the ground. But no, it wasn't cloth at all but a jagged circle of caterpillars—fifty, maybe a hundred—all tangled, woven together. Like a crocheted pot holder. Gold flecks braided through the black.

"Pretty remarkable, huh?" Archie said, and Sky shot him a look, though he didn't seem to notice. *Remarkable* was definitely not the word Sky would've chosen. *Creepy*—that was more like it.

In fact, seeing so many caterpillars together in one spot made her skin tingle, made her think that something was fluttering along the back of her neck. But when she lifted her hand, nothing was there.

"I went to the library and found some local field guides." Archie gestured to a few books, a blue backpack, lying in the grass nearby. "Normally the eastern tent caterpillar doesn't start its migration until mid- to late April."

"Migration?" The word jumped out. "Like birds?"

"Not exactly. But they do travel." Archie knelt down close to the pile, knees sinking into dirt. "In fact, the eastern tent caterpillars can travel up to two miles a day looking for food. Quite a distance, considering their size, wouldn't you say?"

Sky nodded. She couldn't take her eyes off the pile, the living pot holder. It was mesmerizing in a weird way, the whole thing moving without going anywhere, black-and-gold bodies writhing, *undulating*. The word came to her from somewhere, a book she'd read, a vocabulary list she'd gone over with her mother.

"They're not migrating very far right now," she pointed out.

"That's true," Archie admitted. "But this shows how social they are."

"Social?" She knew all about animals like horses being social, never wanting to be alone, but bugs?

"Yes! Apparently they like being together. They like to congregate in a big group."

"Why? I mean . . . how?" She paused, started over. "Do they *talk* to each other? I mean, do they have their own bug language?"

There, now she'd done it. *Bug language?* She waited for Archie to give her that slow-kid look. But he surprised her.

"That's a good question!"

She checked to see if he was joking, but it didn't seem like it.

"Bugs do communitcate in a way. Although, it's not clear exactly how. It may be a pheromone they send out. Or some kind of fluid trail. I've read that a few scout caterpillars go first, looking for food. When they find it, they send back a message, and the rest follow."

"What kind of food?" She had a sudden vision of carnivorous caterpillars taking over the planet, a bad horror movie.

"Other insects, plants. The wild black cherry tree is the main food source for these guys. They love to eat the leaves."

"Oh, yeah." Sky nodded. "You always see lots of webs in wild black cherry trees. But—" She squinted over at the living pot holder. "This group has a long way to go. There aren't any wild black cherry trees around here."

"That's not true." His head swung up. "They're all over Kentucky. I've seen them."

Ah—there it was, the look she'd been waiting for, the tone. Like she wasn't the brightest bulb on the tree.

"There aren't any wild black cherry trees at Shaughnessy," Sky said, carefully, slowly. Maybe she was getting back at him—just a little. "Frank makes sure of that. You never ever want wild black cherry trees on a horse farm. The leaves are poisonous. A horse can die just from eating a few."

Archie's brow had knitted together while she was talking, but now it smoothed. "Oh, I see. Thanks for telling me that." His gray eyes met hers, locked. "I'm sorry I didn't believe you before."

"It's okay." Sky shrugged like it was no big deal. They were silent for a few awkward seconds, but then Archie jumped up.

"I'd like to make a note of that!" He was reaching for the backpack, pulling something out. "This is my field journal." He held up a small black book, hardback but no title on the cover.

"I'm trying to keep track of everything about the eastern tent caterpillar," he explained, kneeling down again, flipping through the pages. "Even the tiniest detail is important when you're doing research."

Sky stepped closer, glanced over Archie's shoulder. The pages were unlined, but the handwriting inside was neat, precise, organized. There were drawings too. Basic but not bad. A couple of butterflies, moths, and then lots of caterpillars.

"Is this for school? A project or something?"

"No, it's just a hobby right now. But I want to be an entomologist when I grow up." He glanced at her. "That's a scientist who studies bugs."

"Oh, right," Sky said, though she'd never actually heard the term before.

"Weird, I know." Archie made the same little grimace. "But I've always been into bugs. I can't explain it, but I have. I guess that makes me a certified nerd." He went back to the journal, took up a pencil wedged between the pages. "Gramps definitely thinks so," he added quietly, more to himself.

Sky remembered how Mr. Mac's voice had changed, how he'd said something about kids needing to spend more time outside.

"He's just really into horses," Sky offered. "The way we all are around here."

"I know." Archie started writing. His hand holding the pencil was so clean, so neat—just like the handwriting. No calluses, no dirt stains. Nails perfectly clipped.

Sky glanced down at her own hands—defintely a few callusses. The fingertips were grass green from being in the field all morning, and some of her nails were ragged. She stuffed her hands into her jeans pockets.

"I could help if you like," she offered. "I could help you figure out how far these guys have to go for food, I guess."

"That's a great idea!" Archie turned to a blank page. "How far is the closest wild black cherry tree, do you think?"

"Um, well . . ." Thinking it through as she spoke. "There

are wild black cherries along the main road, past the front entrance to Shaughnessy. The county doesn't cut them down. Even though they should when they just sprout. Frank says they grow like weeds if you don't keep on top of them."

"And how many miles do you think it is to the main road?" Archie asked.

"Couple of miles, at least." Sky waited while he wrote that down. "Oh!" Snapping her fingers. "I remember Frank telling me that it's cyanide in the wild black cherry leaves. That's what makes them so deadly." She stopped. Could that be right? "But then why don't the caterpillars die? If they eat all those wild black cherry tree leaves?"

"Another good question!" Archie's eyes brightened. "Maybe you want to be an entomologist too?"

"Nah, think I'll stick with horses."

"Probably a good idea," Archie agreed. "Well, I happened to just read about that in one of those books over there. The eastern tent caterpillar has the ability to synthesize cyanide. They digest the poison and then excrete it in their waste."

"Yuck." Sky had never thought about bugs having "waste."

"Well, it's a really tiny amount of waste." Archie went back to writing. Sky glanced over to Poppy, but she was still content.

"I keep the mare log," Sky said, realizing it was something

they had in common. "It's what we use during foaling season to keep track of what's going on with the mares. I keep it updated with any changes."

"That's interesting," Archie said. "What kind of changes?"

"Well . . ." Sky thought about what she'd logged in last. "Temperatures, for one thing. We take temperatures, morning and night. If there's a sudden spike, it usually means the mare's getting ready to foal.

"So there *is* some science involved in foaling, right?"

"Sure . . . ?" She knew he was getting at something, but it wasn't clear.

"Because my grams thinks all you and your father have to do is ask the mares and they'll tell you."

"Well, we—" she began, but Archie interrupted.

"My grams thinks that horses actually talk somehow. She thinks that you and your father can understand what they're saying."

Sky opened her mouth, but no words came out. Did the Macs know their secret? How long had they known? Had someone told them?

"Honestly, I think Grams is getting a little batty in her old age." Archie rolled a finger at his temple—the universal sign for crazy. "I mean, I know that you and your father are really good with horses. I know you probably consider yourselves horse whisperers or something—"

"We don't call ourselves that," Sky blurted, the first thing, out of all Archie had just said, that she could grab on to. She knew there were books, movies, about horse whisperers, but her father had always poked fun at them a little.

"I just mean that—"

"I've been around horses my whole life." Sky was the one to interrupt now. "So has Dad. It's what we know. It's what we . . . *do*." She threw a hand in the air. "It's how we make a living."

"Exactly, but it's not some kind of . . . magic, right? Like Grams thinks. You can't actually hear the horses talking, can you?"

Sky saw right away that it wasn't a question she was supposed to answer. Archie was laughing, and she was supposed to laugh along with him. Talking horses! How silly!

But she couldn't laugh. She felt the familiar heat rising, flooding through her.

"Do you ever get tired of moving around?" A new question, totally different direction. "Never having a proper home?"

"We have a home!"

That did it. The heat was all the way up now, she couldn't stop it. A current was pulsing through her, making her want to turn and run.

"My parents travel a lot too, but they don't always take me with them," Archie was saying. "I wish they did, though. I'm not really liking this school here, and I'd love to get out of going like you do."

"I go to school." The words were quiet, but sharp, and now Archie seemed to realize something was wrong.

"I'm sorry. I didn't mean—" he began, but she was already bolting.

"I've got to go," she said over her shoulder. "I've got chores to do."

"Oh, okay," Archie called out behind her. "I'm sorry, Sky. I hope I didn't—"

But she didn't hear the rest. She was moving fast, striding across the field, clucking to get Poppy moving too.

The mare lifted her head, took a couple of steps toward Sky, then halted. Something was bothering her, Sky could tell instantly. Poppy was puffing out her lips, rolling her tongue, spluttering a little.

"What is it, girl?" Sky ran the rest of the way toward her. "What's wrong?"

Prickles.

That's what Poppy was saying.

Prickles. Bitter. Bad.

"Is it something you ate?" Sky scanned the place where

Poppy had been grazing, but saw only grass, some clover. "What is it, girl? What's the matter?"

Stings.

Sky reached out and gently took hold of Poppy's muzzle. She peered inside the mare's great mouth.

Green saliva, green bits of grass. And chunks of something . . . black-and-gold chunks.

"Caterpillars!"

Sky reached in and plucked at the caterpillar pieces. Then she quickly swiped her fingers down the side of her jeans, went in for more.

"You've chomped some caterpillars along with your snack," Sky explained.

Tastes bad.

"Yeah, I bet they do, nasty things!"

Stings.

"I know, I know," Sky murmured. Because she was getting a stinging sensation now that she was touching Poppy, not strong, but definitely there. She peered into Poppy's mouth again, and that's when she saw a red place, a tiny cut on the side of Poppy's tongue.

"There it is," Sky said. "But it's just a scrape, really small, nothing to worry about." She stroked Poppy's neck. "I know it hurts, though. Sores inside the mouth always hurt more."

She swiped some more caterpillar guts from under the mare's chin. "Let's go back and get you a nice drink of water, and I'll clean it all out."

"Is everything okay?'

Archie, of course. Calling to her. He hadn't moved from his spot. She wondered what he'd thought of her "talking" so much to Poppy.

"Yeah, it's fine," Sky called back. "She just needs a drink, is all. Needs fresh water. She got some caterpillars caught in her mouth and they taste bad."

How do you know they taste bad?

That's what she expected him to say, so she quickly turned and patted Poppy on the rump to get her moving. But something popped into her brain.

Cyanide.

Sky whirled back to Archie.

"Can the caterpillars hurt the horses?" she called out. "Can caterpillars poison horses like wild cherry leaves do?" She'd never heard of such a thing, but the she'd never known about caterpillars eating cyanide either.

Archie stopped, mulled it over. Sky felt her heart speeding up.

"No," he called finally, shaking his head. "It's just a trace amount of cyanide in their bodies—a tiny amount. Not nearly enough to hurt a horse. Horses weigh, what, around a thousand pounds?"

Sky's heart slowed. "At least," she breathed. She put her hand to Poppy again. "It's fine, girl, everything's fine." Because the mare had started to react to Sky's tension, flicking her tail, bobbing her head, and Sky wanted to reassure her.

"We just need to get back to the barn," Sky told her. "Get you a drink." She reached for the bridle, and that's when she noticed the chunks of black and gold still clinging to her fingers. She dropped down right where she was and started swiping her hands across the grass, trying to get rid of the bug guts once and for all.

But the caterpillars were here, too. One, two—no, three. Skinny black bodies weaving slowly through the green blades, golden eyes staring up at her as they went.

Not eyes, she reminded herself. Just spots, camouflage.

"Are you sure you don't need some help?" Archie called then.

"No!"

The word came out sharper than she'd intended.

"I mean, it's okay," she thought to add. "Thanks . . ."

"Sure, it's fine. I guess I'll see you later."

Again, Sky could tell Archie was disappointed, hurt even, but at the moment she didn't care. Her priority was Poppy.

Plus she didn't like what Archie had said—about her not having a proper home, about not going to school. Even about Mrs. Mac being batty—Mrs. Mac was one of her favorite people in the world.

Maybe Sky was overreacting. Fight or flight like usual. But she just wanted to be alone for a while. She didn't want to talk anymore—at least not to humans.

12

Over the next few days and nights, the mares held off foaling, distracted-seeming. But full-on spring arrived anyway.

"Looks like you brought something with you from Florida," Frank said to Sky one day.

"What do you mean?" she asked, suddenly worried.

"The sunshine!" Frank cried, and gave her a funny look. "The warm weather!"

"Oh, right! The sunshine." Acting like she'd known it all along. "Yeah, I guess we did."

Trees started budding, and buttercups ruffled the green fences. Red and yellow tulips framed the entrance to every barn. A carpet of crocuses rolled out across the pastures, purple and bright.

It was beautiful but strange, like Mother Nature was

being tricked into something she shouldn't be doing.

"We're bound to get another cold snap," Frank kept saying. "A full-on freeze, and then all these pretties will get a shock."

But the temperature kept rising all week, and everything flourished, including the bugs. The black flies swarmed the mares like it was the middle of July. And the caterpillars came on like some kind of mini-alien invasion.

Caterpillars stringing their way across the fence planks; caterpillars bunching along the parking lots and walkways, the horse trails. Caterpillars hugging the sides of the barns, the warm metal water tank walls.

"It's almost biblical," Mrs. Mac said during one of the visits to the foaling barn. "A plague of caterpillars."

"Should we spray?" Mr. Mac asked. "Get rid of them all?"

"Don't want any pesticides near the mares this close to foaling," Frank told them. "The tent worms are just a nuisance, is all. No real harm."

"But the mares don't like them. They taste bad," Sky said without thinking. She glanced at Mrs. Mac.

My grams thinks that horses actually talk somehow. She thinks that you and your father can understand what they're saying.

"I mean," Sky started over. "The mares make these terrible faces when they eat the caterpillars while they're grazing. And then they're constantly trying to spit them out."

"Well, I'm not surprised," Mr. Mac joked. "Those critters look like they'd taste terrible."

"But the caterpillars give the mares these little cuts inside their mouths," Sky persisted. Because it wasn't just Poppy. She'd noticed the cuts in the other mares too.

"Cuts, you say?" That got Mr. Mac's attention.

"Cuts," Sky confirmed. "It's because the caterpillars are prickly, not soft like you'd think." She glanced at Mrs. Mac. "Archie taught me that." She wondered if Archie had talked about her after that day in the field. She wondered how much the Macs talked about her and her father in general—their abilities—when they were on their own.

Mr. Mac turned to Sky's father. "Are these cuts something to worry about, James? Are they getting infected?" Mr. Mac waited, but her father had obviously not been paying attention. He was standing right beside them, but he was staring off down the aisle, miles away, Sky could tell.

"James, do you think this is something we should be worried about?" Mr. Mac tried again.

Now James blinked, glanced around, trying to catch up.

"The caterpillars," Sky prompted. "How they bother the

mares. The bad taste, the cuts." She knew she wasn't the only one the horses had complained to.

"Oh, that's nothing," her father said, waving a hand in the air. "Nothing to worry about."

"Sky told us that—" Mrs. Mac began.

"A few little scratches never hurt anything," James said. "The mares just get a bit sensitive right before they foal."

Sky opened her mouth. She knew all about the mares being sensitive, but this seemed different somehow.

"Nothing to worry about," her father repeated, gentle but firm, putting a hand to her shoulder. "Nothing at all."

"All right, then." Mr. Mac gave a quick nod. "All right. Next order of business!"

Sky felt her father's hand pull away. He and Mr. Mac and Frank moved on, but Mrs. Mac stayed back for a moment.

"Thanks for telling us," she said, giving Sky a tight squeeze. "And keep an eye on it for us, will you?"

"Sure."

Sky turned and headed to the office. She felt a little miffed, she couldn't help it. Maybe the cuts were nothing, but her father had never acted like that, dismissing what she had to say. As she walked, though, she let it go. The cats kept distracting her, zooming past, crisscrossing the aisle, swirling at her ankles. Not just Lucy and Gray but a fat tabby named Marshmallow and a young calico named Tootsie.

The cat population had tripled over the last week because most of the mares in this first group had their own feline companion that traveled with them from barn to barn.

Horses like to congregate too.

Something she could've said to Archie if he was there.

Just like your beloved caterpillars.

Horses craved companions, never wanted to be alone. Donkeys were the most common to use as a horse friend, but Sky had seen goats and sheep at other farms. At Shaughnessy it was mostly barn cats.

Now Sky made sure that all the cats had food and water, and then she went into the office, closed the door. She sat down at the desk and scrolled through the mare log. She didn't have anything to add . . . or did she?

She thought of Archie and his notebook, how he'd said that everything was important, even the smallest detail. Shouldn't she make a note about the cuts, the stings?

Her fingers hovered over the keys. She knew her father wouldn't look at the log, or probably wouldn't. He rarely did. But Frank would see it. And so would Gaby and the interns. And the Macs would read it later.

In the end, she pushed the keyboard away, and instead

opened the right-hand drawer where she kept her horse carving and her knife.

The front legs were nearly right, long and graceful, but the back legs were still caught inside a slab of wood. She might be a natural, like Gaby said, but she was slow. Five to one—that was the ratio. Gaby would have a whole box of little horses to send over to Shakertown by the time Sky was done with her first.

"Better get to work, then, don't have all day," Sky muttered to herself, Frank's favorite phrase.

The knife seemed to move of its own accord, freeing one back leg and then the other. She worked for a while without stopping. The office door opened, closed, but she didn't look up.

"Hey," her father said.

"Hey," she answered back.

"Just going to make some coffee. Want some?"

"Nah, I'm okay."

"Mrs. Mac said to tell you bye for now."

Sky nodded. She kept focused on what she was doing. After a while she heard the coffeepot making its final rumble. She heard her father taking out a mug, pouring the coffee.

"Gaby said she was teaching you that." Her father came to stand beside her. Then he sat down in the La-Z-Boy, blowing the steam off the coffee. His hair was tied back in a ponytail, and he'd shaved that morning. He looked better than he had when they'd first arrived, but still rough.

"I'm pretty slow. Gaby's got a box full, and I'm still working on this one." Sky held the horse out, and her father set his mug down on the desk, took the carving in his hand. His fingers were callused, rough. She wondered if his hands had ever been as smooth and neat as Archie's.

"Not bad." Her father nodded. "Not bad at all."

Sky grinned. It felt good. Her father praising her for something. Especially after what had happened with the Macs. She knew he hadn't meant it, not really, just didn't want to upset the owners so close to foaling time.

"The wood is maple," Sky told him now. "It's easy to carve, soft. Gaby got a bunch of it from a friend of hers over in Boyle County. Tree fell down after a big wind. So she has plenty."

He held on to the little horse a moment longer, rubbing a finger along the curves. "Nice," he said, handing it back to Sky.

"Do you know how to whittle?" she asked. "Did anybody ever teach you?"

"Yeah, when I was younger than you. Maybe eight or so." He took a tentative sip of coffee, then a deeper one. "Your great-granda, he's the one who taught me. He was always carving things. Birds mostly—he loved birds."

Mom loved birds too. She loved them so much, she wanted to be one.

That's what went through Sky's head, but she didn't say it.

"What kind of birds?" she asked instead.

"Oh, all kinds. He'd make them small. Miniature. Tiny birds, but detailed as anything."

"And was he one that could talk to horses?"

Her father nodded.

"Did he move around like we do?"

"Of course. The Dorans were born restless," he said. "That's what my granny always told me. All down the line, we've never been rooters."

"Rooters?"

The word caught her.

"A rooter is what my granny called somebody that puts down roots, stays in one place their whole life," James explained.

Sky was quiet, thinking how Archie had said that she and her father didn't really have a home. Was it true? And did it matter?

"Have *you* ever wanted to stay in one place?" Sky asked in a quiet voice. "Put down roots?"

"Have you?"

Sky was surprised. Her father was looking at her, really

looking at her. She felt like he hadn't done that in a long time.

"I don't know," she admitted. "Maybe it would've helped Mom." She regretted saying it as soon as it was out. Her father's eyes—red-rimmed as always—were filling up. "I didn't mean—" she started, but he interrupted.

"I know, luv, I know." He blinked and cleared his throat. "I woulda turned rooter for sure if it would've helped. But everything went so fast."

Sky felt the pressure building behind her own eyes, so she held the horse carving tight in one hand, willing the tears to go away. The front hooves dug into her palm, and it hurt, but it helped, too. Made her stronger.

"Have you ever told anybody about the gift?" Sky asked, since it seemed to be a time she could ask questions.

Her father shook his head. "Had to tell your mother, of course. No secrets between us. And then Frank, well, you know how he is. He just kept pestering me."

Sky rolled her eyes. "I know." She paused. "I just wonder if the Macs know."

"Have you told them?" He was looking straight at her again, and he didn't seem happy this time.

"No! Of course not!" she cried. "It's just . . . we've known them so long." She paused. "They'd probably understand."

James gave a sigh. "Maybe, but you never know. Most folks

get a little wary if you start saying you hear voices. In fact they put your great-granda away when he started telling people about it. Put him in a loony bin. Took him years to get out."

"A loony bin?" Sky didn't think she'd ever heard the word before.

"Loony bin," he repeated. "It's what they used to call a hospital for crazy people." He put a finger to his temple, drew a circle, just like Archie had done, which made Sky laugh.

"Loony bin," she said, laughing still. "It's a funny word."

"Funny *farm*, that's another thing they called it."

And now they were both laughing, and it felt so good, so right, just like old times.

Nothing to worry about.

That's what her father had told the Macs just a little while ago, and maybe it was true.

Nothing to worry about.

Sky wanted to believe it—she *did* believe it. But she slipped a hand under the desk, rapped her knuckles to the wood just the same.

13

One of Sky's daily jobs was hosing down the outside of the foaling barn, keeping the walkways and the entranceways neat and tidy. Usually it was an easy task since everything at Shaughnessy was neat and tidy to begin with. But this year was different.

"Caterpillars sure love blacktop," Sky said to Gray and Lucy as she rolled one of the many hoses from its hook on the wall, pulling it through the main door. "I wonder if Archie has put that detail down in his little book."

The cats said nothing back of course, just yawned. They were lying twined together in a patch of afternoon sun, obviously loving the warmth of the blacktop as much as the caterpillars did. But they both stood and stretched when Sky flipped on the hose. Instead of running away from the water, though, they made a game of it, acting like kittens, batting their paws at the black-and-gold bodies swirling past.

"You don't want to really catch them," Sky said. "They're nasty. Haven't the mares told you?" She assumed cats and horses communicated, but wasn't completely sure.

Sky sprayed down the whole length of the front parking lot, then clicked off the hose and grabbed the push broom. That was her system: hose, then sweep the leftover bodies down the drains that ran along the sides of the barn, then hose again.

In the past she'd only had to do the job once, maybe twice a day, but now she was up to four times between sunrise and sunset, and even that wasn't enough. There seemed to be an endless supply of caterpillars, an endless army marching, or wriggling, across the parking lots, the driveways.

A sea of caterpillars.

That's what it looked like sometimes, when she gazed out across the pastures, like the whole world was moving— *undulating*—and it made the hairs on the back of her neck rise up and tingle.

"Archie must be in bug heaven," Sky said to Mrs. Mac on her next daily visit. Sky hadn't seen Archie at all; she'd look for him when she was out with Poppy. She wondered if he was staying away on purpose or if he was busy.

"Yes, he is!" Mrs. Mac cried. "He's actually started collecting the caterpillars in jars and putting them in a couple of old aquariums we found in the attic." She gave a big fake shudder. "So now we have them inside *and* outside the house."

"Creepy." Sky tried the fake shudder herself. "I get enough of them outside. I wouldn't want them inside too."

"Well, as long as they stay in the aquariums," Mrs. Mac sighed, "I'm okay with it."

"You could tell Archie to come here," Sky said, as Mrs. Mac was leaving. "There's always a caterpillar carpet in the parking lot out front. I keep hosing it off, but it always comes back."

"Caterpillar carpet, that's funny," Mrs. Mac said. "I've taken to calling the aquariums in Archie's room Bug TV because he spends so much time sitting in front of the tanks, staring."

"Bug TV," Sky repeated. "That's funny too."

Mrs. Mac put an arm around Sky's shoulder. "Archie can be a loner of sorts," she said in a confiding voice. "But even loners get lonely sometimes." She tilted her head. "Don't you agree?"

Sky nodded without thinking too much about it, because it seemed like what Mrs. Mac wanted her to do. But later, after the older woman was gone, Sky wondered.

Had Mrs. Mac been talking about Archie? Or had she been talking about Sky, pointing something out?

Of course Sky wasn't a loner. She preferred a herd, just like horses did. In fact she'd be in a herd of horses all day long if she could.

But horses aren't people.

The thought slipped in without warning.

"Horses are better than people."

That's what she said—out loud—even though there was no human about to hear.

14

Sky held off hosing later that day, thinking Archie might come to the barn, but he didn't. She waited till long past the time she figured he'd be out of school, and then she went ahead and cleared the caterpillar carpet.

The next afternoon the carpet was back, just as thick, and she was pulling the hose out the main door as usual when she saw Archie coming her way, blue backpack slung over one shoulder.

"Hi," she called.

"Hello," he called back.

"You got here just in time," she told him, dragging the hose all the way across the courtyard. "I was about to clear this whole lot away—" She stopped short. Would Archie be upset about her killing so many caterpillars? Her mother had hated killing anything, even the smallest spider. What would her mother think of this anyway? Would she be angry about the daily caterpillar massacres, or sad?

"It's fine," Archie said. "They can't *all* live, it's a simple fact. Overcrowding always causes population problems. Not enough food, not enough space, not enough mates. Most of them are starving, actually."

"Starving?" Sky glanced quickly at the black-and-gold bodies near her feet. "How can you tell?"

"Some of them are starting to get weaker. They lose the will to look for food, to travel for it. They start to dry up, and eventually they'll probably just blow away."

"I wish they'd blow away now," Sky muttered, but Archie didn't seem to hear. He'd pulled a mason jar from his backpack and was squatting down so he could scoot a few caterpillars into it.

"Is it for your Bug TV?" Sky asked. "Mrs. Mac told me about the aquariums in your room."

Archie rolled his eyes. "I don't really sit there all day and watch them. She and Gramps only think I do."

He stood and screwed the lid back onto the jar. Sky noticed that he'd already poked holes in the top so the bugs could breathe.

"I'm sorry about rushing off the other day," Sky began.

She'd decided that she needed to apologize, and she wanted to get it over with as quickly and smoothly as possible. "It's just—"

"No, I'm the one who's sorry," Archie told her. "I didn't mean to say you and your dad don't have a home—that was really rude."

"It's fine." Sky gave a small shrug. "We don't, not really."

"Neither do I." Archie took a step forward. "I mean, maybe that's why I brought it up like that. Because my parents are gone, and I'm not exactly sure when they're coming back. I'm not sure if we'll move back to DC all together, or if I'll go to Africa with them. I just don't know. And I usually like school, but like I said, I'm not crazy about this one, and who knows what school I'll be in next." He let out a sigh, studied the jar in his hands. "Anyway, I didn't mean to go into all that. I just wanted to tell you that I'm sorry if I said something stupid the other day."

Sky shifted the hose to one hand. "It must be scary. Not knowing what's happening next."

He nodded. "I like things organized. So, yeah, this has been hard."

"I'm lucky I don't have to keep starting new schools all the time. But I'm probably behind now. I haven't been doing what I'm supposed to be doing."

"I could help sometime. I mean, if you need help. Probably you don't."

"Sure, maybe sometime," Sky told him. "But right now I have to clean all these caterpillars away." She lifted the hose. "So if you want any more Bug TV participants, you'd better go ahead and get them."

"I'm fine. I have enough for now." He started to put the jar away in his backpack. "I'll just be going so you can get your chores done."

"Sure," Sky said, but then she thought about her conversation with Mrs. Mac.

Loner.

Lonely.

"You could stay and help if you wanted," she offered. "But you might not like this chore very much. I'm basically about to commit major caterpillar homicide."

He grinned, shook his head. "I'm okay with it, really," he told her. "Circle of life, and all that."

"Circle of life," Sky echoed. It was something her mother always talked about.

After Archie had put his backpack in the office, Sky explained her system and they started clearing the entrance-ways together. Sky kept checking Archie's face to see if he was really okay with it all. His eyes did seem to take on a mournful sheen as hundreds upon hundreds of soggy caterpillar bodies swirled down the drains. But when she asked if he wanted to stop for a while, he said no.

"They'll be back tomorrow, every one," she told him when they were through. "I promise."

"I'll be back too," Archie said, but then he seemed unsure. "I mean . . . if you need more help."

"Never turn down free help," Sky told him. "Something Frank would say."

"You know, Frank sort of scares me," Archie admitted. "He can seem pretty grumpy sometimes."

"It's all an act," Sky said. "Well, mostly an act. But he's a good guy deep down, the best. He's like a grandpa to me. Especially since I never knew my real ones. They died before I was born."

"On both sides?"

"Well, my mom's mom died when she was little, and then her dad died later, when *I* was little, so I don't really remember him."

"I'm sorry," Archie said, his voice going quiet.

"It's okay. Like I said, I never really knew them."

"No, I mean, I'm sorry about your mom."

Sky stiffened, she couldn't help it.

"I remember meeting her a couple times," Archie said before she could get the dreaded *Thanks* out.

"You do?" Sky was surprised. Archie had been around during foaling season so rarely.

"I remember how pretty she was, and how she had this way of looking at you. Like she really cared what you were saying even if you were a little kid."

"Yeah." Sky nodded. "That's her."

"I think she was coming to see Grams one time, and I was out playing on the porch. I'd found a spider and I had it trapped in an upside-down jar. A really big spider, black, shaggy hair."

"Wolf spider," Sky said, making a face. "I hate those."

"Most people do," Archie told her. "But your mom didn't. She sat right down beside me on the porch and let me tell her all these facts about spiders I'd just learned, and she kept agreeing with me about how great they are."

Sky nodded. She could see the scene exactly. Her mother liked spiders. She'd even had a favorite—the granddaddy long legs. She'd pick one gently up and let it walk along her arm.

"Look it, a little alien!" she'd cry, trying to get Sky to do the same, but she never could. Spiders were just too creepy.

"I remember before she went on in to Grams, she told me to make sure to let the spider go," Archie continued. "Not to keep it too long, and definitely not to kill it."

Sky nodded again. "That was her. She hated killing any-thing. She'd probably hate me killing all these caterpillars."

"I think she'd probably understand since they're so . . . prevalent."

"Yeah, they're prevalent all right." Sky could already see a few scouts, or whatever they were, inching their way back onto the blacktop. "Thanks," she said to Archie, still keeping her eyes on the tiny parade. "Thanks," she repeated, because she really meant it, same as she had with the cats on that first day.

"You're welcome," Archie said.

15

Archie came every day after that; he came when school was through.

At first Sky only asked him to help outside the barn. The hosing down, the sweeping up—the caterpillar massacre. But soon, Archie was helping inside the barn as well. The mares took to him right away, just like Poppy had. Even Floss liked him.

"You should take that as a big compliment," Sky told him. "Floss is particular."

Floss was the only gray in the Shaughnessy line. Her base coat was pearl-colored with darker shades of gray and black dappled through.

"Yeah, Floss is picky. She's never been sure of me," Gaby said one evening when Archie came to help feed the mares during her shift. "She usually hides from me all night long. But as soon as you show up, she's all, 'Look at me! Look at me!'"

"What do you mean, she usually hides?" Archie asked. "How does a horse hide from somebody if they're inside a stall?"

Sky started to try to explain, but Gaby interrupted.

"A horse can do a lot of funny things, especially when they're about to foal. They all start acting strange. Some will get mean and some will get nice. Some will get hungry and some won't touch a bite. Lady Blue, she'll get restless, wanting to pace up and down, be led down the aisle and back again. Some will get still. And sly."

Gaby wagged a finger at Floss. "Like that one there."

"Sly?" Archie asked.

"Most grays get sly, and then they hide in their stalls," Gaby said. "All the way back so I can't see them from the office, can't see them even if I come out in the aisle. Got to go all the way up to the gate to find out what they're doing."

"Just the grays?" Archie asked.

"That's right." Gaby nodded. "It's something my grandpa always told me, and I've seen it myself."

"Is that true?" Archie asked later, as Sky was walking with him back to the Macs after dark. "What Gaby said about grays? Does your father think that too?"

Sky hesitated. Archie had apologized for saying stuff about home and school. But they'd never touched on the whole talking-to-horses thing again.

"Nah. Dad says horses have their own personalities, just like people. They don't act a certain way because of their coloring."

"But does Floss hide, the way Gaby says?"

Sky shrugged. "Horses seem to like to feel safe before they foal. It's true that Floss will scoot all the way back into the stall, kind of wedge herself into one corner, and then it's hard for Gaby to see her from the office. But she's not doing it to hide from Gaby really, it's just what makes her feel safe."

They'd reached the top of a little hill. Sky stopped and looked back the way they'd just come. The fields and sky were black—there didn't seem to be any stars out. But all the windows of the foaling barn were lit up, small bright squares in the dark.

"It looks like a ship," Archie commented. "A ship on the ocean at night."

"Yeah," Sky agreed, thinking of their Florida campground, of the boats gliding by on their way somewhere else. Her mother would always make a game out of guessing where the boats were headed.

"Take a look at this," Archie was saying now, beaming his flashlight down, illuminating a clump of caterpillars—not as big as the living pot holder from before, but pretty impressive.

"Do they ever sleep?" Sky asked, realizing it was a question she'd never thought of before. "Do they *need* sleep?"

"They definitely need rest," Archie answered, "since they travel so far. I believe they go into a sleeplike state."

"You probably know this, but horses can sleep standing up," Sky told him. "I used to try to do that when I was little, but I never could. I'd always tumble over at the last minute."

"I actually sleep with my eyes partially open," Archie said.

"No way."

"It's true. My lids roll up partway when I'm in a deep sleep. It used to freak my mom out when I was younger."

"I can understand why," Sky said. And then another question popped into her head. "What do the caterpillars see? Do they see us?"

"Not really. They sense things, through their antennae on the front, through those prickly hairs. They're very sensitive, apparently."

"Does that mean they can *feel*?" She thought of all those caterpillars she'd blasted down the drain. Had they felt pain?

"Nobody knows for sure," Archie said. "For a long time, scientists didn't think animals could feel. They said animals only mimic human behavior."

"Horses don't just mimic," Sky said.

Archie nodded. "Modern science proved that animals are able to exhibit complex emotions. But there haven't been that many studies on bug feelings. Except there's this one experiment that a bunch of scientists conducted with hungry fruit flies. The scientists wanted to see if the fruit flies felt fear, and so they cast a shadow over a group to mimic an overhead predator."

"What did the fruit flies do?"

"The fruit flies reacted like humans or animals would. When the shadow was there, the fruit flies stayed still, ignoring the food laid out for them. Even after the shadow was gone, the fruit flies waited a long time, ignoring their food, like they were making sure the coast was clear before eating." Archie paused. "They repeated the experiment over and over again, and the fruit flies reacted the same way every time."

Sky leaned toward the circle of light Archie was making and stuck her hand out, blocking part of the beam. The caterpillars were completely still. But then maybe they'd been that way the whole time. She hadn't been paying attention.

"How long do they live?" she asked, pulling her hand away. "I mean, normally? If they don't run into a bunch of grazing horses or a girl with a hose."

"Total life span for the eastern tent caterpillar is about seven to eight weeks."

"Wow, that's pretty short. I'd hate to come back as a caterpillar."

"Come back?"

"Oh." She wrapped her arms around her shoulders, hugging herself. There was a breeze whipping up. "My mom believed in reincarnation." She paused. "You probably think that's silly. Not very logical or scientific. Nothing you can prove."

Archie didn't answer right away. "What did your mom want to be?" he asked finally, and at first Sky didn't want to tell him. It was hers and hers alone.

But then she thought of how little she'd talked about her mother since she'd died. Her father never spoke of her. Sky thought of how Archie had given her that memory of the day with the spider.

"She wanted to be a bird," Sky whispered.

"What kind of bird?"

"An arctic tern."

"Why?"

"Because they see more daylight than any other bird. They travel over twenty-four thousand miles in one year."

"That's just about the circumference of the earth."

Sky nodded. She knew that fact. She wasn't surprised Archie knew it as well.

"An arctic tern lives about twenty-five years usually, and it spends most of its life flying," she told him. And then, without warning, a sob was rushing up and out. Sky turned away from Archie.

"Sorry," she blurted when she could speak, rubbing a hand across her face, glad for the dark night, glad Archie couldn't see her. She started to move on—she'd promised to show Archie a shortcut home—they should get going. But something fluttered along one palm. She almost jerked away, thinking of wriggling caterpillars. But the thing touching her was a hand, not some kind of creepy bug. Archie's hand.

"Even if I did believe in reincarnation, I'm not sure I'd honestly want to be a caterpillar—though it would certainly make for some great research." Archie's hand was warm around hers. "I guess it would depend on if there were any grazing horses or girls with hoses nearby."

Gently he squeezed her fingers and she squeezed back, and then they both dropped hands and started walking again, the flashlight picking out the way.

16

Coming back into the foaling barn later, after she'd walked Archie to his home and back, Sky heard voices echoing down the aisle.

"From where I'm standing she looks like an overstuffed sofa," Frank was saying. He was leaning into Lady Blue's stall, Burley and Gaby standing by.

"Shush, old man," Sky heard her father scold from inside the stall. "No trash talk here. You're disrespecting one of my finest gals."

There was a pause. "Well, I like overstuffed sofas. They're comfortable."

Gaby let out a laugh, and when Sky came up, Gaby draped an arm over her shoulders.

"What's going on?" Sky asked, heart speeding up just a little. Was it time? Was a foal finally coming?

"Our Lady is feeling a little achy tonight, I guess," Gaby said. "All that weight she's been carrying."

Sky nodded. She could sense the dull but constant pain now that she was just a few feet away. It was pulsing out of Lady Blue's back hip, the place that always gave her trouble during foaling, ever since she'd torn a ligament in a race years ago. But Sky's father was there, hand on the exact spot, massaging, working at the pain, trying to get it to release.

"Should be tonight for sure, don't you think?" Frank said, but her father didn't answer. "She's leaking already. I can see it from here. Don't want that colostrum to go to waste."

Colostrum was what came first, before the milk. It was packed with so much of what the foal needed right away—vitamins and protein and stuff to boost the immune system.

Sky crouched down, holding on to the bars of the gate, peeking through. She could see some of the yellow liquid flowing out of the udders, streaming down Lady Blue's thigh.

"Wonder if the milk will be tainted?" Frank said.

"Tainted?" Sky glanced up at Frank.

"Might could be." He pursed his lips. "All those caterpillars mixed in with the grass they eat."

"But . . . I thought you said the caterpillars were just a nuisance," Sky said.

"Well, I've seen it before—a mare's milk going bad when too much of something gets mixed in with their regular feed." Frank scratched his head. "I'd hate to pay four hundred dollars a pint if those foals reject their own mama's milk!"

"Four hundred dollars?" Sky asked.

"That's what Thoroughbred milk goes for if you have to buy it from the vet."

Sky blinked. It was hard to believe something so basic would cost so much. But then if a foal didn't get colostrum right away, it was bad news.

"You worry too much, old man," Sky heard her father toss out.

"Maybe *you* don't worry enough," Frank replied.

Sky heard her father grunt, but then he bent over, swiped some of the leaking yellow liquid onto his fingers, and took a sniff.

"I'm going back to check on Floss," Gaby announced. "She's hiding again, since little Mac isn't here."

"I don't think he likes that nickname very much," Sky said.

"You don't see him around at the moment, do you?" Gaby gave Sky a pointed look and then mouthed the words, "He's kinda cute," before walking off down the aisle, glancing back long enough for Sky to shake her head in response.

"Anyway, I'm betting on tonight," Frank said. "Lady Blue

needs to get that foal out of her. It's been long enough."

"Long enough," Sky echoed, because it was true.

A mare keeps a foal safe inside her belly for nearly a whole year—three hundred and forty days, give or take. So it's not just a tiny thing by that time, but a mini-horse basically. Standing within the hour, running soon after.

"Can I help?" Sky asked suddenly, needing to get closer to Lady Blue, closer to her father, too.

James seemed to hesitate, which was strange, but Frank was already unlatching the gate.

Lady Blue's pain pulsed out at Sky as she came near. Sky placed her hand next to her father's, the horse's pain throbbing down her arm. When she was little, she'd jerk her hand away, frightened. But now she knew what to do. She started rubbing the flesh the way her father had taught her, and after a few minutes the ache began to ease.

"That's it," her father murmured. "That's right."

So Sky moved in closer, and he let her take over. She started rubbing in a circle, slowly, skimming the muscle and then pressing into it. Fingers first and then knuckles, kneading the pain away.

"Good girl," he said, and then he stumbled, leaning for a moment against her shoulder. "Just a little clumsy," he mumbled, and that's when she knew.

Her hand froze and she stared at her father, but he did not meet her eye, would not.

Why?

That's what was in her head. What she wanted to ask out loud.

Why? Why? Why?

But she couldn't say a word.

Lady Blue sensed something was wrong. She reared back. "It's okay," Sky whispered to the mare. "I'm sorry I scared you. It's okay, but I've got to go." She put a hand out to make sure Lady Blue was steadied, then turned to the gate, eyes down. She couldn't look at her father.

"What's the matter?" Frank asked. "What's going on?"

Sky took a breath. Now would be the time to come clean, to tell Frank everything. Now, before the mares started foaling. Before she and her father and Gaby and Frank were knee-deep in the weeds. Now would be the time to tell.

"I'm not feeling so good," Sky heard herself say. Not a total lie. She had started trembling, and her stomach was clenched tight as a fist.

"You do look kinda wonky. Here, let me see." Frank put the back of his hand, papery and cool, to her forehead. "And you're a little warm." He clicked his tongue, gestured down the aisle. "Go on, go get some rest." His voice was gruff, but his eyes were soft. "I'll need all hands on deck soon enough. Tonight maybe."

Sky nodded. "I'll be fine later," she told him. "I'll be fine." She walked straight to the Doran Suite without looking back. But when she made it inside, she didn't go to her own room but headed through her father's door.

17

It's not like she hadn't known what was going on with her father back in Florida in the weeks after her mother had died. You can't grow up around horse people—tracks and trainers and grooms and jockeys and owners—without knowing a drunk or two.

But before her mother's death, Sky had never actually seen her father take a drop of liquor. Ever.

The first night he'd disappeared, a couple of weeks after her mother had died, Sky woke up in the dark and knew she was alone. When she checked her father's room, the bed was empty.

Sky had wrapped one of her mother's sweaters around her shoulders and headed down the path to the beach. Staring at the ocean—day or night—had become a main pastime, so she thought she'd find him down by the water's edge.

But her father wasn't there; the beach was empty.

She trudged back and forth, one way and then the other, calling for him. But the wind kept swallowing her voice, and the moon had gone behind some clouds. It was inky black, the air too cold for just the sweater.

She thought she'd wait in the kitchen nook until he came home—sit and wait. But she must've fallen asleep, one cheek flat on the table.

A bunch of sounds jolted her awake—the door banged open too hard, boots heavy on the metal stairs, a body slamming into the kitchen cabinets, knocking a pan to the floor with a loud *clang*.

She froze—too scared to move at first, too scared to speak.

The dark shape stomping into the trailer didn't sound like her father, didn't smell like him either.

Even when he wasn't spending every day in a barn, her father still kept the scent of horses about him: hay and oats and grass and earth. A bit of salt as well, since they'd been at the ocean for so long.

But there was something else mixed in now, something sweet, though not in a good way. A sickly sweet, almost rotten.

Sky rose up fast, tugging the sweater around her, peering into the dark.

"Maggie May?"

It was her father's voice. A wave of relief swept over her.

"Maggie May?"

Sky took a step forward. "It's me, Dad. It's me." She waited for him to laugh at his mistake. But he stepped back, leaned into the wall behind him. He put both hands to his face, and then he slumped to the floor.

"I'm sorry," he whispered. "I'm sorry."

It took a while for her to get him to bed. It was like he'd suddenly gained a ton of weight and lost his sense of balance—all at once. Finally, she got him there, took his boots off, and covered him with a sheet.

"I'm sorry, Sky, my luv," he said, taking her hands. "I'm so, so sorry."

Over and over again.

"It won't happen again, luv. I promise you."

But it did.

Not the very next night, but the one after that, and the one after that, and on and on.

Sky stopped waiting up for him, stopped looking for him in the middle of the night. Stopped jumping out of bed at the first sound of his clattering.

During the day they hardly spoke. Her father slept mostly, or just sat on the beach, staring out. The food ran low, so she started walking the two miles to the Speed-Away to get what little the dwindling wad of money stashed in one of her father's old boots would buy: bread, peanut butter and jelly, some canned soup, macaroni and cheese.

Sky started counting the days until they usually headed to Shaughnessy. But the date passed and her father didn't show any sign of hooking the truck to the trailer.

That's when the cell phone started ringing. She wanted to answer, but her father always had it in his pocket—even when he was passed out for the night. All Sky could do was listen as it rang on and on. Finally it stopped for good—the battery gone dead, she knew.

Sky wanted to call Frank herself. She knew that's who was trying to reach them, to find out when they were coming. But the Speed-Away pay phone had been busted for months, and the new guy behind the counter gave her the creeps. There'd been other folks in their campground, old couples mainly, that she'd known for years. But they'd all moved on for the season by that point.

Sky started thinking she could maybe do the hitching herself if she got the truck backed up a certain way. Maybe she could start driving while her father was sleeping. She'd been behind the wheel plenty of times—maybe not on the highway, just on the farms they worked. But still.

Lucky for Sky it didn't come to that. One day she woke

up and her father was doing what she'd been scheming: He was hooking the truck to the trailer, getting them ready to go. He hadn't shaved, but he'd showered the sickly sweet smell away. Soon as he'd finished stowing the outdoor things, they got into the truck without a word and headed north.

18

Sky checked her father's boots first. It's where he'd always
hide an extra stash of money if they had it; it's where she'd
found the little bottles the first time, back on the beach.

But tonight the boots were empty. So she moved on to
the jackets and shirts, sliding the hangers quickly, reaching
into the pockets.

If she found anything, she'd pour it down the sink—she'd
done that once in Florida. She paused a couple of times to
make sure no one was coming. Once she thought for sure
her father was there, but it was just the mares, the usual
stomping, pawing, getting settled for the night.

Sky was about to give up, a final check of the very back
of the closet, when she caught a faint whiff of something so
familiar it hurt.

Gardenias.

Her mother's scent. Gone from this place, from every-where. Returned somehow. Faint but distinct.

Sky raked the hangers back, and there it was: her mother's favorite shirt. A light blue madras with silver stitching at the collar, bird shapes. A souvenir from India, where she'd traveled before meeting James Doran, before having a daughter.

Sky just stood staring for a moment. She'd done a whole load of laundry only yesterday. She'd put her father's clothes away herself. And this shirt had definitely not been here. It should be in the trailer, all the way at the back of the farm, packed in a box like everything else that had belonged to her mother.

Why?

That's what she wondered. And then: *Why not?*

She walked all the way inside the closet, put her nose to the shirt, inhaled deeply, and her mother was there with her, telling her how everything was going to be fine.

But that was the first time. After the first doctor visit. When they thought one operation and some chemo would do the trick. But it hadn't. Not at all.

Sky reached up and tugged at the sleeves of the shirt, tugged them tight around her shoulders. And then she closed her eyes and pretended, pretended that it was her mother's arms, not just lifeless cotton, her mother's arms, holding her close.

You've got to be strong, Sky.

That's what her mother had said before she died.

You've got to be extra strong. For your dad.

And Sky had promised even though she hadn't understood, not really. Her father had always been strong. What could possibly change? What *had* changed?

Sky's eyes popped open. She really did hear footsteps this time, coming down the aisle, outside the main door to the Doran Suite. She pushed the shirts back into place and got ready to rush out into the bathroom, just around the corner.

But the footsteps didn't stop, they kept on going down the aisle—Gaby or Frank or her father, she couldn't tell which, checking on the mares.

Sky closed the closet door behind her and went to her own room. She was suddenly so tired, she could hardly keep her eyes open. Her arms and legs were heavy, weighted down. But she made herself put on her pajamas, laying her clothes out along the bottom of the bed like she always did—ready for a quick change if the foaling started.

She was just about to get under the covers when something made her return to her father's room. Listening for footsteps, she pushed open the closet once more and took the blue madras from its hanger, hurried back to bed.

The scent was fading from her mother's shirt already, so Sky did the only thing she could think of: She slipped the shirt over her head, pulling it into place. And then she lay back and let her eyes finally fall shut.

She was in a garden of flowers, fragrant and soft, gardenias, all of them surrounding her, everything else fading away. She didn't know how long she was gone—forever, it felt like—but then a voice was pulling her back.

"Sky. Sky, honey."

Was her mother in the garden with her?

"Sky, Sky, wake up."

Was her mother staring down at her, eyes bright in the dark?

"Sky, hon, wake up. I need some help. It's time."

No, it was Gaby, not her mother. Gaby, leaning close, gently shaking one of her shoulders, calling her name.

"Sky! Sky, are you awake?"

"Yeah," Sky answered, trying to blink the foggy sleep away. "Who is it? Which mare?" Because she knew that's what Gaby had come for. One of the mares was foaling.

"Lady Blue." Gaby gave her shoulder a final shake. "You really awake, hon? You coming?"

"Yes, I'm awake!" Sky sat up. "I'm coming!"

Gaby moved to the door. "Good girl."

Sky's heart started beating faster. Her hands shook a little with a sudden rush of adrenaline as she reached for her jeans. This was it! This was what they had been waiting for!

"Wait!" Sky called. "Dad there already?"

Gaby didn't answer, didn't look back, and that's when Sky knew. But she had to ask the question anyway.

"Is Dad with Lady Blue?"

"No, hon," Gaby said, and Sky could hear the worry in her voice, could hear the effort to hide it. "I don't know where your father is."

19

Closer to the stalls, Sky felt the agitation. Like a storm building, a pressure in the air.

The mares, all of them, were wide awake and watchful. Some were pacing in circles, others were standing stock-still at their gates, heads held high, alert, noses twitching.

"Shush-shush-shush," Sky murmured as she hurried down the aisle. "Shush-shush-shush. Nothing to get worried about, nothing at all. Everything's gonna be fine."

She kept murmuring the phrase like a mantra, over and over again, calling it out louder to the mares as she went into the storage room to wash her hands with the special antibiotic soap. She kept repeating the words—steady and calm—even though inside her guts were churning.

Where is Dad? Where is he?

The question spun, a loop inside her head.

Where did he go? Where would he be?

Back in Florida, he'd wander the beach, the place Sky's mother had loved, for hours in the dark. But here, where would he go? Back to the trailer? To get more of her shirts, more things to hold on to?

Or into town? A liquor store, since Sky hadn't found any bottles in his room.

"Sky, you there?" Gaby's voice echoed from down the aisle, Lady Blue's stall. "Are you in the storeroom?"

"Yes, I'm here!" Sky yelled back.

"Bring the supply cart! Hurry!"

"Got it!" Sky grabbed the plastic cart, its drawers filled with foaling supplies, and rolled it as fast as it would go down the aisle.

The moment she entered the stall, it hit her. Pain. Like a bucket of cold water dumped over her head.

Sky stopped to get her balance, catch her breath.

I'm used to this.

That's what she told herself. Because it was true. She'd felt this her whole life. She understood what pain did to the mares, how it scattered their thoughts, made them frantic. All she had to do was calm them down, make them feel safe. It didn't matter that her father wasn't here. She knew exactly what to do.

"You're going to be fine, Lady Blue," Sky said, placing a hand on the mare's neck, damp with sweat. "It's all going to be fine."

"I called Frank," Gaby told her. "He's on his way."

"Good," Sky said, though, was that good? Frank would be so angry!

"In the meantime, why don't you help me wrap her tail," Gaby instructed, and so Sky reached for the supply cart and grabbed a bandage from the top drawer. Then she went to Lady Blue's rear end and gently but firmly took hold of her tail so that Gaby could start winding the bandage around the thick black hair.

Tails were wrapped so that the hair would be out of the way of the foal coming. But it had to be done right—too loose and things would be messy; too tight and the hair would actually fall out later, the horse going tailless for a few months.

"There we go!" Sky said when it was neat and tidy. Then she went to Lady Blue's front again. "What do you need, luv?" she asked straight out, looking her in the eye. Because a mare as experienced as Lady Blue knows exactly what she wants, Sky had learned that pretty early on.

Keep moving. Got to keep moving.

That's what Lady Blue was saying, so Sky took hold of

her halter and walked her in a circle inside the stall.

Once, twice, three times.

Lie down!

The order came urgent, fast.

"You sure, girl?" Sky was surprised. Lying down is what a mare wants to do when she's just about ready to foal, and Sky didn't think they were that far along yet.

Down. Now.

The need was loud and clear.

"Okay, girl, okay."

Sky nodded to Gaby, and they both backed out of the way so Lady Blue could ease herself down into the soft clean straw. The mare let out a grunt deep in her throat and rolled off to one side, legs kicking out in front of her, enormous belly rising up like a mound of dirt.

"We better check her," Gaby said, reaching for the supply cart. "Even though James isn't here. We better check her now."

Sky glanced over her shoulder. Surely her father would arrive any second. Surely he hadn't disappeared completely, not when he'd just been helping Lady Blue a few hours ago, not when he knew how much pain she'd been in, how close she'd seemed to foaling.

"I'll do it," Sky said as calmly as she could. "I'll check her."

"Are you sure?"

Sky heard the hesitation in Gaby's voice.

"I do it all the time," Sky told her. Which was true. It's just that her father was usually there as well.

"Okay." Gaby nodded, pushing past the doubt. "Okay. And then I'll check her too."

They switched places, and Gaby knelt down and started cooing to Lady Blue, a soft, singsong voice, words of comfort and strength. At the same time she reached one hand into her pocket for her cell phone.

"Thought Frank would be here by now," she muttered, punching a button.

Sky took a deep breath. Her hands were shaking, but just a tiny bit.

You can do this.

That's what she told herself, and then she reached into the supply cart and pulled out a long latex glove, rolled it on, nearly to her armpit.

"I'm going to check you now," Sky said as she kneeled down behind Lady Blue. "You're going to be fine."

Lady Blue gave another low grunt, but she kept still, and Sky pulled back the wrapped tail and took another deep breath.

Once her hand was in place, she closed her eyes so she could concentrate on what she was feeling: a tunnel, impossibly small and tight. Her hand kept moving down, gentle but firm, down, down, down until her fingers grazed something hard.

The foal's hoof!

"How are we doing? How's she feeling?"

It was Frank. He'd come up behind her, leaning down to her level, hands on knees.

"The hoof," she whispered, glancing at him, then closing her eyes again. "One hoof."

"That's great. What else? Take your time."

Sky pushed her hand farther down. "I've got the nose, the head. . . ." She paused for a moment, then pushed on again. She knew she had to find the other hoof.

"There it is!" she cried, and she felt a hand on her own shoulder. "The other front hoof."

"Good job, girly!" Frank said. "You're doing great."

Sky smiled thinly. She knew from all the times she'd done this with her father that position is everything in foaling. When you're checking inside a mare, you have to find one hoof and then the head tucked close. And then the other hoof, poised and ready to go, as if the foal is about to step over a divide, which of course is exactly what it's doing.

Unborn to born.

Finding one hoof without the other is bad news. Or finding two hooves and then the head way back is trouble. Both meant that the foal had to be coached into position, which could be hard on the mare.

"So, where's your dad, Sky?" Frank asked the question she'd been dreading.

"I don't know." She kept her eyes shut tight. "I'm sorry, Frank, I don't know."

Frank put a hand to her shoulder. "Well, we've got one Doran here," he said, squeezing. "And that's better than none."

She opened her eyes and realized Frank was watching her intently. He believed in her, she could tell. But still, he was worried. He got up, pulled out his phone, and went out into the aisle. He was calling the Macs, most likely, giving them an update. They'd want to be here. They tried to be here for every arrival, no matter when it happened.

"Everything feeling okay in there?" Frank asked when he came back into the stall. "Everything feeling right?"

"Everything's great," Sky answered. She started to ease her arm back out, but then she remembered. She had to give the foal a little nudge first.

And so she did it. She nudged the tip of the foal's nose with her pointer finger and waited.

Nothing.

Which wasn't all that strange. Sometimes a foal could be slow to respond.

Sky was about to nudge again, but there was a commotion, and her father was bursting into the room.

Sky felt relief washing over her like a wave in the ocean, sudden and strong, and she waited for him to put on a glove and kneel down in the straw beside her.

"Tell me, Sky," he said, "tell me what you've got."

The relief vanished, the wave going out.

Her father's shoulder leaned into hers, and the smell rolling off him was terrible, ugly. Blasting out plain as day—no hiding it, no hiding *from* it. No way to block it out.

"James Doran!" Frank's voice was sharp behind her. "What the blazes is going on? Where in the world have you been?"

Sky shut her eyes tight. She had to concentrate, had to ignore the noise around her. She took a deep breath and pushed at the foal's nose again, pushed and waited.

Nothing.

And that's when a tingling started, right at the base of her neck.

"Dad," she whispered, and he was close, he was there, smell or no.

"Talk to me, Sky," he said. "Tell me what's happening."

"He's not . . ." Sky was certain it was a colt now, a male foal, though she didn't know exactly how she knew. She opened her eyes, stared at her father. "He's not . . ."

"Move," he ordered, and when she hesitated—everything going blurry for a second—he said it louder, "Move!"

The word jolted her into focus again, and Sky pulled back, sliding her arm out and falling backward into the straw.

In an instant she had righted herself, yanking the glove down her arm, leaving it behind her. She moved along the floor on her hands and knees, moved to Lady Blue's back, placing her palms flat against the curve.

The pain was bad, but, strangely, Lady Blue wasn't doing anything about it. Wasn't trying to roll the pain away, kick it out of her. She was just lying there, barely moving at all, calm as anything.

Sky glanced at her father, but she couldn't read his expression. His hair had fallen forward, covering his face.

"Everything's going to be okay," she said to Lady Blue, because it was all she could do. And because it was true, wasn't it? Nothing bad ever happened, not with the Dorans around. Mr. Mac had said so himself.

But one of the Dorans *hadn't* been around, not when this had started. And maybe that's what had triggered something, triggered the bad luck, waved it down from where it had been hovering. Maybe her father being gone had allowed the bad luck to seep in, work its way past the green barrier.

Suddenly Sky wanted her father's St. Christopher medal, wanted it around her own neck. Wanted the carving too, the little horse she'd started but still hadn't finished—why *hadn't* she finished it yet, why *had* she been so slow?

Screeeeeeeeeeee!

Lady Blue finally made a sound, and it was loud and terrible. Like nothing Sky had heard before.

Screeeeeeeeeeee!

The mare's neck arched backward, and a spasm passed through her body.

Screeeeeeeeee!

And then Sky heard another sound: a familiar wet ripping. And her father was falling backward into the straw, bringing something with him as he went. The foal of course—dark and wet. And still.

For a moment nobody moved, nobody said a word, but then her father was yelling, "Get the oxygen tank!" and Sky was scrambling up, rushing to the cart. She reached into the bottom drawer, the one they'd hardly ever needed. The oxygen mask was awkward, slippery, in her hands; she couldn't seem to pull it out. But Frank was there, yanking at the thing, handing it over to her father.

Sky took a step forward, but that was all she could do. She watched her father kneel down over the unmoving foal, slide the mask over its small wet muzzle and tug at the straps, cinching them tight.

"Come on," he whispered. "Come on, luv."

Sky hugged herself. She was cold again, so cold. Cold and shivering.

"Come on!" her father said, louder this time. But nothing happened, nothing changed.

So he was ripping the mask off again, holding the foal's mouth closed. He was leaning down and putting his own mouth flat against the nostrils, trying to blow his own breath into the foal.

The shivering had taken over. Sky was shaking full out now, teeth chattering together. She understood that time was passing, but she didn't know how much. She knew that time was an enemy, knew it deep in her soul.

"Come on!" her father kept shouting. He kept repeating the same motions, over and over again.

Fitting the mask onto the tiny muzzle, taking it off again. Bending down and blowing breath into the colt. Waiting, listening.

Starting it all again. Over and over and over.

"Leave it," Frank said at last. "Leave it, James!"

Sky watched the old man reach out and grab hold of the oxygen tank, wrench it from her father's grip.

"Leave it, son! The foal is dead."

And that's when the shivers took over completely. Sky's legs were too wobbly to hold her up any longer, and she sank to her knees in the straw.

20

It's a rule of foaling that once one mare goes, the rest are sure to follow. And that's just what happened.

First Darsha, and then Marigold and Dulcimer. Miss Lynn and Penny.

The night stretched on and the day opened up and the sun got swallowed again by another chunk of darkness.

And the foals just kept coming—all of them perfectly formed, all of them perfectly still.

With Floss's filly there was some hope. She came out breathing but weak. They wrapped the preemie blanket around her little body and tried to keep her warm. She took a bit of her dam's milk but spit it up again right away. Within the hour she was gone, just like the rest.

Gaby never left, even when her shift was over. And other people kept showing up too—Wick and the grooms Javier and Cesar. The Macs of course—Archie, too, at least for a little while. She couldn't look any of the Macs in the eye. She knew they all must blame her, blame her father for the dead foals.

At some point the vet arrived and there was talk of quarantining the first group of six mares on one side of the foaling barn, separating out the other twelve. After that he'd need to examine all the mares—the ones in the east barn as well—to see who was still carrying a live foal, who was not.

Poppy!

Sky couldn't believe she hadn't thought of Poppy till that moment. She'd been so caught up in what was happening here. But now she had to get to Poppy. She started down the aisle, but someone stopped her.

"You can't go to the other barn, Sky." It was Frank, holding her arm.

"But Poppy—" Sky began.

"You can't go there yet," Frank said. "I'm sorry. But we can't take the risk. In case it's contagious, whatever this is. We're going to have to scrub down before we go to the other barns. All of us. We've got to wait till the vet says it's safe."

"Okay." Sky nodded to show she understood, but she couldn't look Frank in the eye, same as with the Macs.

"Okay," she repeated, and then, "How's Poppy? Who's over there with her?"

"Ross and Victor. The mares are fine right now. They're fine."

Sky nodded again. Poppy loved both Ross and Victor.

"Good girl." Frank squeezed her arm, then let it go. She turned—not sure where to head next, but needing to be busy, helpful.

That's when she saw her father, striding her way. She waited, sure he was coming to hug her, hold her. Comfort her. They'd hardly spoken, except when he'd given orders, telling her what to do next.

"What's this?" His voice was sharp. And his hand wasn't reaching for her after all, but for the shirt she was wearing. His fingers plucked at the fabric. "Where'd you find it? What are you wearing it for?"

Sky glanced down, realizing she hadn't changed tops when Gaby had come for her last night—or the night before? When was it? She'd lost track of time.

And she'd lost track of the shirt. It was ruined—splotched with dirt and darker stains, blood of course. Mare's blood. Sky was covered in it.

"I'm sorry," she said, trying to brush at the blood, brush it away—stupid of course, it was dried in. "I'm sorry." The stains went blurry, tears filling her eyes. She looked up at her father, something coming clear.

"This is our fault," she whispered. "This is all our fault. The bad luck followed us. It followed us here." She gazed past him all the way down the aisle. So many mares. She could feel them, though she couldn't see them all. She could feel their pain.

"Where were you anyway?" She focused on her father again. "Where were you when Lady Blue started foaling?"

Her father seemed startled by the question. He was looking at her—finally—looking at *her*, not her mother's shirt.

"Where were you?" she asked again, nearly shouting this time. "Where were you?"

Her father's eyes were bloodshot, red-rimmed like they'd been for months. They'd been red for so long. Crying for her mother, crying for the mares. So much to cry over. But suddenly it didn't matter. Somehow his crying made Sky angry instead of sad.

"Where were you?" she shouted. And then she did something she'd never done before, never thought to do. She pushed her father.

"Where were you?"

He stumbled, caught himself. But she was on him right away, thrusting her arms out again.

"Where were you?"

He didn't fall back this time, but stood, unyielding. And for some reason it made her want to push again, so she did. She pushed and pushed, and when he didn't stumble, she kept on going.

Her father's arms fell to his sides and his chin came down, messy black hair covering his whole face. But otherwise he didn't move, didn't yield. Didn't speak or cry out, didn't tell her to stop.

And so she kept pushing harder and harder. Because he wasn't flinching, wasn't falling. Like he was so tough, so strong. But it wasn't true. He wasn't strong at all.

"How could you leave them when they needed you? How could you leave the mares? How could you leave them?" Over and over, pushing, pushing, until the sentence changed. "How could you leave me? How could you leave *me*?"

That's when she stopped. She backed away, chest heaving. Then she turned and fled down the aisle, passing all the mares inside their stalls, the pain and sorrow pulsing out to her as she ran. She passed the vet and Gaby and the grooms, and she kept going until she was inside the Doran Suite, inside her own room.

She jerked out of her dirty, bloody clothes, left them in a pile on the floor. And then she threw herself onto the bed, pulling the covers over her head, burrowing down into a hole.

Instantly she fell into a deep, dark sleep, and if she dreamed at all, she never remembered. The dreams were gone when she finally woke up nearly twenty-four hours later. The dreams were gone, and so was her father.

Part Two

MYSTERIOUS TRAGEDY STRIKES THE BLUEGRASS

LEXINGTON, KY.—Across the fields of bluegrass, the mystery of what has been tragically killing off this year's crop of Thoroughbred foals at an alarming rate finds countless volunteers taking on the role of detective and painstakingly combing pastures where the suspects range from a deadly fungus in the hay to bacteria in the soil to this year's unusual infestation of the eastern tent caterpillar.

Scientists from the top equine centers, agronomists from all over the state, and owners and managers of local brood-mare farms have banded together to uncover the mystery syndrome that has caused at least 500 mares to deliver stillborn or dying foals.

"In all my years, I've never seen anything like this," says

Archibald MacIntyre, II, owner of Shaughnessy Farms, which has been breeding top Thoroughbreds for over a century. "Shaughnessy was hit hard, and I want to know why. We went into this foaling season blind, and we won't do that again. We need to understand what's happening before we even think about breeding for next year. Losing foals like we did, well, it's a terrible, terrible thing to witness."

"We're working around the clock," says Todd Brady, who is directing the volunteer teams laboring at the rate of a half-day per pasture painstakingly searching, clipping, and sampling grass, dirt, and hay, and sending those samples to labs here in Lexington. "We will get to the bottom of this, I promise you that."

21

She saw them every time she closed her eyes. The foals. Not just Shaughnessy's, but every single one. A whole line, a parade. Standing nose to tail. Stretching off into the distance.

Five hundred foals.

The number wasn't easy to hold on to.

Five hundred foals.

How far back would a parade like that go? How many fields would it cover? Two? Maybe three? Sky didn't want to do the math but couldn't help it.

If your average foal is almost three feet long—nose to tail—and there are five hundred foals, then the line would go on at least fifteen hundred feet. Which would be about a quarter mile—the distance from the foaling barn to the place in the middle of the field where Sky was kneeling.

Five hundred foals.

Sky gazed back over her shoulder. As if they'd really be there, lined up, single file behind her.

Five hundred foals.

"Are you okay?"

It was Archie.

Are you okay?

The same question everybody had asked. Over and over again. Five hundred times at least.

"I don't know."

The same thing she'd answered. Over and over again. Five hundred times at least. The best she could do.

I don't know.

Foals were dead, or dying. Her father was gone. He'd left a note saying he was sorry but he'd be back soon, he had to fix something. He'd asked Frank to take care of Sky, and so she'd moved into his cottage. But she wasn't sure who was taking care of who.

Sky had never seen the old man this way. All the gruff pushed out of him, so that he seemed even older than before. He didn't growl or bark anymore, just talked in a thin, old-man's voice. And he was prone to stopping halfway through a sentence, his words just choked off. The old red hanky pulled out and brushed across his face.

"We're almost done with this area. We'll be able to take a

break soon," Archie was saying, so Sky turned her head from the imaginary parade of horses and went back to spooning a scoop of dirt into a plastic cup.

It's what they'd been doing for days. Going out into the fields. Collecting dirt and grass, putting it into plastic cups provided by the state. Sealing them and marking them, sending them to the research center in Lexington.

It was Sky and Archie, but others too. Not just from Shaughnessy but from everywhere.

"We came when we heard the news," a volunteer from Indiana told Sky the day before. "We came as soon as they said they needed extra hands. We couldn't stand the thought of so many foals dying and nobody knowing why."

I know why.

That's what she wanted to say. To that volunteer. To Archie and the Macs and Frank and everybody.

I know why.

Bad luck, terrible luck. Clinging like smoke. Following the Dorans up from Florida after the death of Sky's mother, spreading everywhere. Despite the lucky green fence, despite the St. Christopher medal, despite Sky's nearly finished wooden horse.

The newspapers said it could be something deadly in the grass or the dirt, something that had festered in the hay because of the warm weather.

Or it might have to do with the caterpillars, because of the high numbers, the cyanide laced inside their bodies, a trace amount multiplied by thousands.

Right now, though, nobody knew anything for sure.

Except Sky.

"I think it's really great how well organized this all is." Archie was talking again. "The volunteers, the kits to put our samples in. Don't you think so?"

Sky didn't answer. She knew Archie was just trying to be normal, to get her to talk. She wasn't talking much lately. But all at once his cheerfulness was like a finger pressing at a bruise.

"You must like this," she said. "It's one big science project."

Archie stayed silent. Sky felt terrible, ugly. But she couldn't help it. Frank had lost his bark, and Sky had claimed it. Everything made her want to growl.

"I don't like why we have to do this," Archie said at last. "But yes, I do like the idea of finding a logical explanation for what's happened."

"What if it isn't logical?"

"It has to be."

The way he said it, so calm, so sure, made Sky want to scream. Instead she took the cup she was holding and rolled it over a lone caterpillar that had strayed into her path, smashing the black-and-gold body.

She didn't know what was wrong with her. She'd never been this way.

But then she'd never lost so much before.

Mom.

Dad.

The foals.

Poppy.

They'd taken Poppy along with the last of the late mares to the special horse hospital in town. They were keeping them there, monitoring the foals. The foals were still alive inside their mamas' bellies. But probably not for long.

They'd taken Poppy away in a trailer, and Sky hadn't even gone to see her, to explain what was happening. Hadn't gone to the special horse hospital to help get her settled. To tell her everything was going to be okay. Because Sky knew she'd be lying.

"Life isn't always *logical*," she said to Archie now, trying her hardest not to sound as ugly as she felt. "It isn't always *scientific*."

She grabbed up the plastic cups she'd filled and stuffed them into the canvas bag they'd been given to use. And then she took off.

22

In a normal foaling season, they would have rotated all fifty-two mares through the foaling barn as they gave birth, moving them on to the two weanling barns, where the mares would nurse and care for their young until the colts and fillies were weaned and separated a few months later.

Of course, this was no normal foaling season.

The mares stayed where they were, divided among the foaling barn, the main barn, and the east barn, their udders filled. But with no foals to take the milk, the mares cried with pain until the vet came to give them shots to dry up the milk.

The mares in the foaling barn kept their same stalls, but Gaby had put up new cards just below the usual name tags, words written in black marker.

DROPPED FOAL.

Sky thought the phrase was almost funny when she first saw it. Funny and awful, both at once.

DROPPED FOAL.

As if a mare had arms to begin with. As if she'd just casually dropped her foal into the straw and all they had to do was scoop him up and give him a kiss on the head to make everything better.

DROPPED FOAL.

The cards were all the same. Not really for Sky or Frank or Gaby, of course—how could they forget?—but for the vets who visited, the scientists from Lexington who came to collect the data.

As always, Sky tried not to see the tags as she went down the aisle, but it was nearly impossible.

PENNY

DROPPED FOAL (COLT)

FLOSS

DROPPED FOAL (FILLY)

DULCIMER

DROPPED FOAL (FILLY)

LADY BLUE

DROPPED FOAL (COLT)

She stopped at Lady Blue's stall because Gray was there in her new usual spot. Actually perched on top of Lady Blue as if the cat was about to go for a ride. Balanced perfectly on the mare's back, the middle of her rump—the widest part.

All the barn cats had stayed in the foaling barn along with their particular mare friend. They'd curl in the corners of the stall to sleep during the day, prowl the gate or sit watch in the stall window. So far none had perched right on top like Gray was doing.

"Crazy cat," Sky murmured, letting herself into the stall, putting a hand to Lady Blue. She worked her way gently down Lady Blue's spine, all the way to where Gray was settled.

The cat opened her bright yellow eyes slowly and stared, deep in purr mode. Sky could feel the heavy vibration through Lady Blue.

"Magic cat," Sky revised. Because it was obvious what the purring was doing to Lady Blue.

The maiden mares had had it easiest. They'd felt the discomfort of full udders. An instinct had told them something was wrong. But they couldn't miss what they didn't know.

Lady Blue was different. She had memories of earlier times, of nursing, of nudging foals to stand on wobbly legs, of taking them out to the pasture. Of running, a shadow keeping pace beside her.

It didn't matter what Sky told the mare, what she whispered while she groomed her. Each time they turned Lady

Blue out, she sniffed at the air, trying to find a scent she knew should be there. She ran from one side of the pasture to the other, trumpeting out her special mama call. Swiveling her ears, listening for a response.

All this was starting to go away. But a tension was still there. An anxious sadness. And Gray was helping, Sky could feel it.

She put both hands on Lady Blue's side, right below where Gray was sitting, and shut her eyes, allowing the rhythmic purring to calm her too. She wished Archie was here to see the cat this way. She wished he was here so she could apologize.

"That's quite a sight."

Frank's voice, not Archie's. He'd come up to the gate, Burley at his ankle.

"She's helping," Sky explained, and when Burley waddled beneath the gate to join her, she saw his sad brown eyes and wondered what he felt. "I bet you want to help too," she said. "But I'm not sure you'd fit up here."

"Now that would *really* be a sight," Frank said. "A sausage riding a mare."

"Who are you calling a sausage?" Sky murmured as Burley flopped over, inviting her to scratch his belly.

"I should fry him up sometime. He'd feed the whole farm."

"That's gross!" Sky said to Frank, and then to Burley, "He doesn't mean it."

"He'd be pretty tough, anyway," Frank mumbled. Then he cocked his head. "Thought you were out helping the volunteers."

"Came in early," Sky answered.

"I can see that for myself." He clicked his tongue, and Burley rolled over—surprisingly fast for how round he was—and ducked back under the gate. "Something for you on the desk."

"What is it?"

"It came in the mail. Something from your dad."

Sky felt her pulse quicken, but she didn't let it show. "So?"

The note hadn't said where her father was going, only that he'd be back. But she'd told herself she didn't care. She was angry at him, ashamed too.

"So, go take a look," Frank said, tapping the top of the gate and moving off, Burley doing his best to follow.

Sky rested her hands where they'd been before, on Lady Blue, just below Gray's puffball body. The purring had stopped. Instead the cat was methodically cleaning one leg. But after a moment she stopped and stared directly at Sky, eyes round and unblinking.

"Okay, okay," Sky sighed. "I'm going."

The office was empty since it was afternoon. Gaby was still coming in for the night shift even though she didn't have to. There was nothing to watch now, but she couldn't shake the schedule, and the Macs had told her they'd finish out the months they'd contracted her for.

The envelope was brown, small, and padded, and her father's handwriting was big and bold—all uppercase letters like usual. No return address, and she was glad. She flipped the envelope quickly over so she couldn't glimpse the postmark.

She ripped at one edge, and something fell right away, something small, wrapped in a white Kleenex. She knew what it was before she pulled the tissue away.

A bird. Maybe an inch long. Rough carved, basic. No details. Impossible to tell what kind it was.

She clicked her tongue, impatient, then closed her fingers over the carving, made a fist.

The bird was light, weightless, barely there. She could toss it into the garbage can next to the desk; she could throw the whole package away.

She was about to do just that when something else slipped from the envelope. A thin rectangle of paper. Folded over, Sky's name written on one side in big letters, all caps.

SKY

She could tell there was writing inside the note, could see the black ink, the tall letters, bleeding through.

She pulled at the handle of the left-hand drawer without looking, the place where she'd kept her horse carving, her knife. She hadn't been able to open the drawer since the foals had died, hadn't been able to touch the thing she'd meant to be her good-luck charm.

She dropped the note into the drawer, let the bird fall too. Banged the drawer closed. She took the envelope and shoved it down into the trash, below some old newspapers and food wrappers so she wouldn't be tempted to look at it later, so Frank wouldn't casually see it. Then she got up and walked out of the office.

23

The call came in the middle of the night like it always did.

Poppy was foaling at the special horse hospital.

Frank woke Sky up, told her that he and the Macs were going, said to get dressed. But she shook her head, pulling the covers over her head.

"The vets'll take care of her," she mumbled.

And they did. Poppy was fine. That's what Frank said when he returned. And so was Juniper. Both had birthed fillies. Small and weak like all the rest. But still alive.

Not for long.

That's what Sky told herself. Because she knew. There was no point in getting any kind of hope up.

It turned out a few foals from other farms had survived too. A handful. She'd read about it in the newspapers, heard about it on TV—because it was a big story, always on the local news. But they were all sickly, no guarantee they'd thrive on their own once they left the hospital.

"I'm heading over," Frank said on the second day. "Come along with me."

"No point," she replied, and she could feel Frank wanting to say something, but he didn't.

After he was gone, she set to organizing and cleaning all the tack in the foaling barn. Which was stupid. Everything was beyond perfect, neat and smooth and gleaming. Frank and Gaby—everybody—had had the same idea. Keeping their hands busy when there was so little real work to do.

But she took out the whole kit—the sponges, rags, saddle soap, neat's-foot oil, and leather conditioner. She went and filled a bucket with hot water, then settled on the floor of the tack room with a bunch of bridles spread out around her.

She loved the smell of tack leather almost as much as she loved the smell of horses themselves. She took the first bridle apart, undoing the buckles and laying the leather strips in front of her. She put the bit into the hot water to soak while she worked at each piece, soaping, oiling, conditioning.

When all that was done, she put the whole thing back together, hung the bridle on the wall where it belonged, and moved on to the next.

She was on her fourth bridle when she sensed someone standing in the doorway behind her.

"I was out with the volunteers," Archie said. "The main organizer came by. Mr. Brady. He said they are finished with Shaughnessy. At least for now."

She nodded, kept on oiling the strip of leather she was holding. "That's good." She wanted to say *sorry*. But she couldn't get the word out, not today. The calmness Gray had given her was gone.

"What are you doing out of school?" she asked instead.

"It's Saturday."

"Oh, right." She still had trouble keeping track of time. Actual days of the week didn't seem to matter.

"Can I help with that?" Archie asked, and Sky shrugged.

"It's just busywork. Not really that important."

"I don't mind."

"Okay, then." She nodded to the bucket. "I've got to change the water out first, though. It's gotten cold, and it needs to be hot."

"I'll do it," he said, setting his backpack on the floor and lifting the bucket, heading for the door.

"Thanks. You'll need to grab an extra sponge!" she called after him. "And a couple of soft rags, too. It's all labeled on the shelves, you'll see them."

"Got it," Archie called back.

When he returned, he settled on the floor directly across from her, legs crossed.

"Here's what you do," Sky said, showing him how to release the buckles, pull the bridle apart, one strip at a time.

"Kind of like a puzzle," he commented. "The tricky part is putting it back together, I assume?"

"Yep, but you'll get the hang of it, I bet," she said, trying to soften her voice, trying to act less angry. It wasn't Archie she was mad at, after all. "And if you don't, I'll show you."

"Sounds good," Archie said.

They worked in silence. Archie was awkward with the buckles at first, his fingers not used to handling tack. But he learned quickly, like she had predicted.

"Hey, I've been meaning to tell you something," Archie said after a while. "You know that day I first saw you? When you were riding Poppy?"

Hearing the name stabbed at Sky, but she tried to ignore it.

"And I told Grams and Gramps that we'd just seen each other from a distance?"

Sky nodded. She wasn't sure why he was bringing that up—water under a bridge.

"I've wanted to tell you . . . I meant to tell you right away but I didn't." He took a breath. "I lied to my grandparents that day in the barn when we first met to protect *myself*, not you."

Sky put the strip down. "What do you mean?"

"I thought I was the one who would get in trouble, not you."

"Why would you get in trouble? You're a Mac. It's your farm. Plus, Mr. Mac *wanted* you to be outside."

"Yes, but he'd just told me not to go into the field with all the mares. Not on my own. He said I might get hurt or I might hurt the mares."

"Well, you *did* almost get trampled to death."

She'd said it deadpan, but she meant it as a joke. Archie would know that, right? She glanced into his face, and saw that he did.

"Anyway," he continued. "I wanted you to know that I was trying to save my own skin, not yours. I was just hoping you'd go along with it."

"Good thing I did." Another joke, another glance. Archie was giving the Mac smile, a little tentative but there.

"I wanted to tell you something else too." Archie's lips fell to a straight line. He hesitated, but seemed to make a decision. "I began to spy on you after that."

"What?" Sky wasn't sure she heard him right. "What do you mean?"

"Well, I . . . used my binoculars . . . to find you in whatever field you were in." His words were speeding up. "And then I'd follow you."

"Why?"

"I just . . ." Color was creeping up Archie's neck, spreading across his cheeks—Sky could actually see the pink taking over. She wasn't sure she'd ever *seen* such a deep blush; she'd only known what one *felt* like.

"I guess I was lonely," Archie admitted. "I haven't really made any friends at my new school. Grams kept talking about you before you got here, and I wanted to meet you again. But then I kept making you angry—"

"I wasn't really angry. I guess I can overreact sometimes."

"Well, you had a right to be angry. I kept saying the wrong thing. I didn't mean to, but I'm not really very good at making friends, if you want to know the truth." He picked up a buckle, ran a finger over it. "I guess I can sound like a know-it-all sometimes."

"Well, you do know a lot." Sky gave him that. "But you don't know everything." Sky closed her eyes, took a deep breath, opened them again. "I have something to tell you, too."

Loony bin, loony bin!

The words popped into her head, a cuckoo clock going off, the little bird poking itself out and back. But she decided to ignore it.

"I *can* talk to horses," she told him. "Just like your grams believes. I can understand what they're saying, I can hear their thoughts, feel what they're feeling. My dad can do it too. It's something that gets passed down through our particular family, one per generation. And it got passed to me." She took another breath. "I can talk to horses."

There. It was done. She'd told someone about her gift, her secret.

But she couldn't look at Archie now. She studied the strip in her hand.

"Wow," she heard him say. "That's really . . ."

She waited for him to use words like *untrue, illogical, unscientific.*

"Remarkable," Archie finished, and she blinked up at him.

"I didn't think you'd believe me!" she cried. "You can't prove it."

"Well . . ." Archie began. "Remember when you asked how caterpillars know to send out scouts? How they know to follow? How they know to congregate?"

Sky nodded.

"And remember how I said that we don't really know how they communicate, but it's obvious they do somehow."

Sky saw where this was going.

"I don't know how you communicate with horses, but

what you do is special, different. I've been . . . watching . . . you, so I've seen it myself." He gave the usual grimace, then cocked his head. "Maybe you could tell me about it."

And so she did.

She told him how she didn't understand it at first when she was really little and how she'd cry then because she couldn't explain what the horse was telling her. She told him how she felt a buzzing when she was even a field away from any horse, and how it got stronger and more specific as she got closer to the horse. She told him how she couldn't hear the foals before they were born, so she hadn't known something was wrong.

"And the mares seemed fine. They didn't seem sick." The words were tumbling out now. "They didn't complain about anything, anything at all. So we didn't know. But it doesn't matter because we *should've* known. So it's our fault, no matter what. Because Dad wasn't paying attention. He was . . . my dad was drinking." She slapped the strip against the hardwood floor. "He was *drinking*."

There it was. The other deep secret she'd kept locked away. It was out now, free. She'd given Archie everything, not just bits and pieces. She'd given him the whole picture, the whole Sky.

But she didn't know what would come next. She thought

about bolting, jumping up and rushing out the door.

"It's not your fault, Sky," she heard Archie say. She felt his fingers wrap around hers, tightening, holding her in place.

"It's not your fault," Archie repeated. "None of it. Your dad drinking—you had no control over that. And what happened with the foals, it's happening everywhere, other farms, not just here."

Sky shook her head. He still didn't understand. Not completely. He didn't know how strong bad luck could be, how it could cling. He didn't know how bad luck could trail a person, a family, how it could find you even when you thought you were free and clear. Seeping out, tainting everything.

"I believe you, though, Sky." Archie squeezed her fingers again. "I believe that you communicate somehow with the horses. Even if it isn't exactly . . . logical."

Sky felt tears pricking her eyes. It shouldn't have mattered what Archie thought or didn't think. But it did.

"Thanks," she whispered.

"You're welcome." Archie smiled. Then he went serious. "Do you remember anything different with the mares, anything at all?"

"No, nothing." Sky shook her head. "They were fine. The usual aches and pains, but nothing really bad, nothing unusual."

Archie let go of her hand and stretched over to grab his backpack. He pulled out the little black book—his field journal.

"It's an empty one," he told her. "I haven't used it yet. I always keep a spare." He held it out.

Sky didn't take it right away. She wasn't sure what Archie wanted exactly.

"It's for you," he said. "Just start jotting down anything you remember—anything at all. That's what scientists do. They take notes to help figure things out. Put down everything. You never know what might be important."

Sky reached for the journal, held it in her hands.

"Okay," she said, even though she wasn't at all sure that writing notes in a little black book would do any good.

24

Prickly. Stings. Tongue too big. Hard to swallow. More stinging.

A collection of words, feelings, sensations. Not just Lady Blue but all of them.

It took a while. Going from stall to stall. Leading each mare back through time with a tidbit to focus on. The day they went to the pond for an impromptu bath; the day Sky took them to the spring house for the shade. Listening to the memories, sorting through the images.

Prickly. Stings. Tongue too big. Hard to swallow. More stinging.

"Is it there now?" Sky asked. The final question. "Do you feel all that now?"

No.

Sky checked every mouth just to be sure, every tongue.

She remembered the rough places she'd felt. Nothing there now. All of it smoothed over.

Prickly. Stings. Tongue too big. Hard to swallow. More stinging.

But the sensations were there. Inside every mare's memory of the days leading up to foaling. It had to mean something.

Sky wrote it down in Archie's black book. She stared at the words.

Prickly. Stings. Tongue too big. Hard to swallow. More stinging.

It had to mean something.

25

Two more packages arrived, one right after the other. Frank left them on the desk again.

Sky went through the same ritual. Turning the envelope over, not looking at the postmark as she ripped one side open.

The second bird was still rough. But the third was a lot better. She could see how the head pointed into a crest. She could see the outline of tiny feathers, the wings. A cardinal, that's what it was going to be. The Kentucky state bird. She could tell even though it was plain wood, not painted bright red.

Sky shoved the folded letters into the desk right away so she wouldn't be tempted to read them. The birds she held on to a little longer. They were tiny in her hand, but they felt heavier than the other carvings somehow, like the wood was different even though it wasn't. It was exactly the same.

26

That night Frank and Sky ate in silence at the table in his kitchen like they'd been doing lately. She knew he was disappointed in her for not going to see Poppy and Juniper, she could feel it. But he'd made her favorite spaghetti just the same, and after Sky had cleaned up ("I cook, you clean" was the rule in his house), she thanked him.

"You're welcome." He was in the living room, lying back in his La-Z-Boy, staring off into space. Burley was curled in his lap.

Sky knew he'd been at the horse hospital all day, knew she should ask about the mares, the fillies. But she couldn't, and yet she couldn't leave the room either. So she lingered, stopping to look at his wall of fame, as he called it.

Photos and news clippings going way back, showing Frank as a grinning young man, all decked out in his jockey silks—lots of different colors since he rode for lots of different owners back then.

Most were action shots: Frank's small, wiry frame perched atop some giant racehorse in the middle of a tight pack; Frank and his horse edging their way out to the finish line; Frank trying to see through mud-splattered goggles on a stormy track; Frank making a victory lap, nearly standing straight up in the saddle with both arms high in the air.

Some were posed stills: Frank and his horse in the winner's circle, grinning from ear to ear, both horse and rider draped in capes of roses.

"Frank the Bank." That's what people used to call him in the old days. Because having Frank Massey ride your horse was like having money in the bank, a sure thing.

"I used to want to be a jockey," Sky said, gazing at one of the grainy victory shots. "Just like you."

"Yeah, I remember. But you got too tall too fast." He grunted. "You wouldn't want that life anyway. It's a rough way of making a buck. Broke nearly every bone in my body, some of 'em twice."

"Even with all your lucky charms?" She'd gotten past the photos, on to the trophies and medals. She stopped at the old cigar box. It was packed full of Frank's lucky charms, the ones he'd used and discarded over the years. Sky knew them all, nearly without looking, by touch.

A pinch of dirt from a lucky track sealed inside a tiny glass vial. A worn sliver of horse's hoof—over fifty years old—from Mighty Heart, his first winning horse.

"Lucky charms don't do a thing," Frank muttered. "Not one blessed thing."

"That's not what you always told me."

She picked up a small felt pouch, knotted, and she didn't have to open it to know what was inside: a snow-white curl of Frank's beloved grandma's hair. He always said it kept him safe, even after she was gone.

"Well, you learn a thing or two when you get to be as old as I am," Frank said now. "And what I've learned, good-luck charms are like those fake pills they give people when they're doing some kind of study. Placebos, I think they're called. Half the folks they're watching think they've taken the pills, and they believe they're going to get cured of whatever ails them. And so they do, they get cured. But in the end all they've really done is take a bit of sugar, a bit of nothing."

Sky put the pouch back into the box and turned. "Dad's always believed—" she began, but he cut her off.

"I know what James Doran believes!" The growl startled her—she hadn't heard it in over a week. "Bad luck finding you and following you." The growl startled Burley, too. He shifted and sniffed up at his master.

"Bad luck clinging," Frank continued, still gruff but stroking the dog to settle him. "Clinging like smoke from a cigarette."

"And that's exactly what happened!" Sky was growling too now. She could be as tough as any old man, tougher. "We've had some pretty terrible luck, you can't deny that."

"I can't deny it, girly! I can't deny you were dealt a rotten hand!" He peered at her, blue eyes fierce. "But it's how you play that hand that makes you who and what you are."

"And how am I supposed to play it?" she demanded. She suddenly wanted to hit something, sweep all Frank's lucky charms from the shelf. "When my own dad takes off? Runs away. Disappears, leaving Shaughnessy and the mares. Leaving me. Going off, who knows where?"

Frank held one hand up. "I'm not saying what James did was right. I was mad at him; so were the Macs. But I believe he was blinded by grief, and he's trying to make it good, trying to get straight." He pointed a finger at her. "And you know where he is, girl, you're getting his letters."

Sky glanced away. She thought about the envelopes she'd stuffed into the trash, the slips of folded paper she'd tucked into a drawer. She'd *wanted* to read them. She missed her father so much. But she was angry at him too.

"You haven't read them," Frank said, realizing it as he spoke. "Otherwise you'd know he's right—"

"I don't care where he is!" Sky cried out, knowing it wasn't true but saying it anyway. "I don't care one bit!"

She rushed past the old man, done with talking. She went straight to the spare room she'd been staying in. She slammed the door and sat on the edge of the mattress, hands clenched into fists.

She didn't think she'd cry. She was too angry. At Frank, at her father, at the world. Why was life so unfair? Why had her mother gotten sick and died? Why had her father started drinking? Why had the foals been too weak to survive?

Why? Why? Why?

The tears came and she didn't stop them. A few drops bringing the flood, just like her mother had always said.

She rolled onto one side, tucked herself into a ball. And then she let it come. All the tears she hadn't cried yet. Tears for her mother, for herself. Tears for the mares and all those foals—those precious foals—five hundred and counting.

She cried till her eyes were nearly puffed shut and her chest hurt. She cried till she was dry as a husk. Then she unclenched herself and lay flat, staring up at the ceiling.

The light from the moon was bright, slashed in a rectangle

across the white plaster. There was a crack in the middle, a fine line right above the bed that she'd never noticed before. It didn't run straight but curved a little—just enough to become a horse, the gentle swell of the neck, rising up from the back. Poppy's back.

Sky wiped her face with a corner of the sheet. Then she walked into the living room and stood in front of Frank. He was still settled back in his La-Z-Boy, eyes closed.

"I want to go see Poppy." Her voice was loud in the stillness.

Frank's eyes popped open. "What, *now?*" He stared at her like she was an alien from Mars.

"Now," she told him.

He clicked his tongue, shook his head. But he was already reaching for the lever on the side of his chair, holding on to Burley as he jolted himself upright.

"Well, give an old man a minute," he said, gruff but resigned. "I'm sure not as quick as I used to be."

27

Sky had always heard about the special horse hospital just outside of Lexington. Bright and Butler, it was called. But she'd never actually been there.

At night from a distance, driving in from the highway, it was like a ship—same as with the foaling barn. But a bigger ship, more modern, all glass and steel.

Frank had called ahead to say they were on the way. He signed in at a desk, and even though it was late, they weren't alone. People were coming and going, same as at a human hospital. Some of the faces were familiar—owners and trainers from other farms. Frank nodded his hellos as they passed.

To Sky it was a maze. But Frank knew the way. They went out of the main building through a long glass hallway into another. They passed waiting rooms and observation rooms—all of them empty this time of night but full of sparkling stainless steel equipment, state of the art, all of it horse size.

Finally Sky started sensing horses, not just steel and glass. She got that buzzing and it grew stronger as they went deeper into the heart of the building.

A girl with short brown hair came forward dressed in blue scrubs.

"Hello, Frank," she said, and Sky realized she was a lot older than she looked. "You must be Sky." She reached out to shake her hand. They were nearly the same height. "I'm Dr. Nash."

Sky nodded, distracted. She could feel the mares, but she could also hear them now. She recognized Shaker Rose's voice and Callabee's, and they weren't happy. They were distressed, worried, calling out—not to her. She cocked her head to catch the sound better.

They were calling out to Poppy. They were trying to comfort her. And Poppy was frantic.

Sky started toward the sound, but Dr. Nash blocked her.

"I've got to get to Poppy. I've got to see her," she explained. "I've waited too long!"

"I understand," Dr. Nash told her. "But you've got to change first. We don't want any outside germs infecting the foals especially."

It seemed to take forever—the changing into blue bubble top and pants and booties. The scrubbing of hands. Sky was like a pressure cooker, something simmering inside her ready to blow the top off. Finally the vet led her down the hall.

Sky paused for Shaker Rose and Callabee. They calmed as soon as they saw her, stepping to the gate and touching their noses to her palm, breathing her in, trying to tell her everything at once. Thoughts rushing out, feelings—all of them confused and sad and angry.

"I'll be back," Sky promised. "I've got to go to Poppy now."

And they agreed. Something was wrong and they didn't like it, didn't understand. They would've broken the walls down to get to her, to protect one of their own, one of their herd, but they couldn't. They were disturbed, but they were dozy too. They must have been given something to calm them down.

"I'll be back," she repeated, and then she pushed past Dr. Nash and Frank and ran the rest of the way down the hall.

Poppy was in the last stall. She was wildness itself, rushing back and forth, pacing at high speed between the walls, head whipping side to side, mane and tail whipping too.

"I think you better wait till she's calmer," Dr. Nash was saying, but Sky barely registered the words. She pushed at the gate and was inside the stall before a hand could stop her.

Poppy was flinging herself around inside the small space, completely out of her mind. She didn't even notice Sky at first. But then she sensed *human*, and her head swung around fast—she wasn't happy with humans just then—and that's when she saw Sky and stopped. Just like that, she stopped.

"Poppy," Sky whispered. "Poppy." She stood and waited for the mare to be angry, waited for a kick or a bite, something hurtful, and Sky wouldn't blame her at all.

She had abandoned Poppy. She'd stayed at Shaughnessy, a turtle inside its shell. She'd let the horse she loved most in the world, suffer all the pain and confusion of being somewhere new alone.

"I'm sorry," Sky whispered. "I'm so sorry."

Poppy's chest was heaving, her whole body bright with sweat, legs lathered. Her eyes were mostly white, the brown nearly rolled all the way back. She kept her head high, nostrils flared.

Sky took a step forward. She held her hand out, and for a moment Poppy eyed it like it was something foreign, something dangerous, and Sky waited for a chomping, teeth against her skin. Instead she felt the soft touch of Poppy's muzzle, velvet and warm.

Here.

That's what Poppy was saying.

You are here.

And Sky felt a release from the mare. Of anger, of worry. Not completely. A lot of it was still there. But part of it melted at touching Sky. Slowly, carefully, Sky moved closer and put her arms up and around Poppy's neck, hugging her like she always did. And Poppy responded by tucking her head down, nodding Sky against her broad chest.

"I'm sorry," Sky said again, and she could sense Poppy's understanding of the word, her acceptance of what saying the words out loud meant. She could feel the comfort she was giving Poppy, how the comfort was releasing some of the tension, some of the fear. Not all of it, of course.

Gone! Gone! Taken!

That's what was still rippling beneath the relief of seeing Sky.

Where? Where? Where?

Sky eased herself from the hug and whipped around to the gate, where not just Frank and Dr. Nash were watching her but a few other vets, all staring as if they'd never seen a girl hug a horse before.

"Where is the filly?" Sky demanded.

Dr. Nash was the one to speak up. "She's in a special ICU stall. She was too weak to nurse. We've been tube feeding her."

Sky had never had to tube feed any animal before, but she knew the drill. You have to get a tube down their throat, all the way to their stomach, without accidentally going into the lungs and puncturing anything. It wasn't easy, but this was a big-deal hospital. They'd know what they were doing.

"Okay, Poppy," Sky said, turning back to the mare. "Your filly is okay right now. She's in another stall. They're feeding her in a special way, to make sure she gets enough. She's okay right now. I'll stay with you now. I'll stay right here."

But Poppy had other ideas. She nudged at Sky's shoulder, nudged Sky toward the gate.

Go.

That's what she was saying.

Go now.

And Sky knew what Poppy wanted her to do. She wanted her to go to her baby.

Sky started to shake her head. She didn't want to leave Poppy now that she was finally there, didn't want to go down the hall. She knew she wasn't strong enough to watch another foal fade and die.

But Poppy nudged at her, nose to shoulder, like she always did when urging Sky to do something Sky didn't really want to do.

"Okay, Poppy, I'll go. I promise I'll help her," Sky finally said.

It was another promise made to another mother, and probably she'd fail, since she didn't think she was very good at keeping promises. But she had to try with Poppy's filly, she knew it. Because it's what Poppy most needed.

28

A bag of bones lying in the corner of a padded stall—that's all the filly appeared to be. Tubes sticking out from her skinny body—not so different from Sky's mother toward the end, and that's what made it even harder for Sky to walk through the gate.

But she imagined Poppy behind her, nudging her forward, and before she knew it, she was kneeling down right in front of the bitty thing.

The filly didn't move, didn't lift her head to check Sky out the way most foals would do. She was curled in on herself, head tucked, eyes closed. Ears flopped completely forward—a bad sign.

A foal's ears should be perky right after they're born, and Sky had seen enough floppy ears over the past few weeks to last a lifetime.

"Hey, girl," Sky whispered, inching closer. "Hey."

The filly was asleep, but Sky couldn't sense any dreams, couldn't sense any thoughts at all. The filly was breathing— Sky could see how the tiny rib cage was rising ever so slightly. But she couldn't *hear* the filly, couldn't get any sense of her, and the tiny hope she'd tried to grasp on to was pulling away.

So she just started talking, rambling the way she always did when she first returned to Shaughnessy, to Poppy. She told about coming through the gate for the first time, seeing how beautiful and perfect everything was. She told about watching for a first glimpse of horses.

"Gorgeous, every one of them," Sky said. "Just like you're going to be one day."

And then she described the fence, the exact color green, the swell of pride she always got when gazing at it.

"It's lucky green," Sky said, even though she wasn't sure about that anymore, wasn't sure about what Frank had told her either—lucky charms being like sugar pills. But she said it anyway, and lots more. She talked about the Macs and Archie, how she wasn't sure she liked him at first, but now she did.

"I guess he's my best friend," Sky told the filly. "My best *human* friend."

And then she was talking about her father because she couldn't help it. She was full with missing him. She described him the way he used to be: handsome and strong, black eyes bright with love for her mother, love for her.

"You'll see. You'll meet him," Sky whispered, and that's when she realized the baby was watching her, had been watching her for who knows how long.

"Hello, girl," Sky whispered. "Hello."

The filly had her head propped across her skinny front legs, dark eyes fixed on Sky.

"Hello, little one. I didn't know you were awake."

The filly blinked, extra long lashes clasping together.

"Hello there."

She didn't startle when Sky leaned even closer; didn't pull away.

I know you.

That's what the filly was saying—her first real words, thoughts, coming through to Sky.

I know you.

Sky reached out, touched Poppy's filly for the first time. A jolt went through her, a current passing between them, strong as lightning, strong as love.

"I know you, too," Sky said. "And I'm going to do whatever it takes to make you well."

29

Just like before, Sky's day went back to starting halfway through her night, and just like before, it was a relief.

First off Sky would see to all the mares in the foaling barn. And then either the Macs or Frank would run her to Bright and Butler, and she'd spend the rest of the day there.

She'd wait while Dr. Nash or one of the assistant vets pumped Poppy's milk into a bottle so Sky could try to feed it to the filly.

"Is it tainted?" she'd asked the first time, remembering what Frank had said.

"No, we've tested it," Dr. Nash told her. "The milk's fine."

Even so, the filly didn't take it. Sky would sit with her for hours, coaxing her into getting some milk down. She didn't have much of a reflex to suck, which was weird. Most of the colts or fillies Sky knew came out with a strong drive to nurse, to get nourished so they could run and then run some more.

"Juniper's filly isn't so bad," she said to Dr. Nash one day, because she'd spent time with her as well. Juniper's filly was still too weak to stand and nurse, but she could take a bottle just fine.

"That's true," Dr. Nash said. "But many of the MRLS foals have been the same."

"MR what?" Sky asked.

"That's what the scientists at the research center have named what's going on," Dr. Nash explained. "Mare Reproductive Loss Syndrome. It's a mouthful, so MRLS for short."

Sky gulped. "They know what's causing it? Nobody told me!"

"No," Dr. Nash said quickly. "They don't know. But they named it so we'd all be on the same page."

Sky bit the inside of her cheek. Who cared about naming something when no one knew how to stop it?

"Hey there, girl," Sky cooed as she let herself into Poppy's filly's stall. As usual now, she perked up at the sound of Sky's voice.

Sky sat down and thought about how to get the filly to take the bottle. But it just wasn't working, and she started to understand from what the filly was thinking, from what she was doing, that it had something to do with her tongue. The filly didn't seem to know which way to hold her tongue when something was inside her mouth—it rolled off to one side instead of staying under the nipple like normal. Sky thought of her father, wondering what he would do, and that's when she had an idea.

"She needs a softer nipple," Sky told Dr. Nash when the doctor came by on her rounds. "She just can't latch on to this one."

Instead of scoffing, the vet went looking for a different nipple in the supply room.

"Hmmm, that's the only kind we have," Dr. Nash reported.

So Sky had Frank stop at a feed store they knew on the way back to Shaughnessy that night. Sky chose two different nipples, both made for baby goats or lambs, rather than horses, but much softer than the usual cow or horse nipple.

"Here you go, girl," Sky told the filly the next morning. "This should be easier to hold on to."

And it was. The filly was finally able to get some milk on her own.

"That's it!" Sky encouraged. "That's how you get more of this stuff that tastes so good. And you want to get more. So you can get strong. So you can get some right from your mama, from Poppy. She's waiting for you to get stronger so you can nurse and be together."

The first bottle went down, and right away the filly was perking up, standing on her skinny legs rather than just collapsing, nudging at Sky for more milk.

"Wow," Dr. Nash said when she came in later. "I don't know why we didn't think of that." She checked the chart. "She's definitely gained some weight. Maybe we're over the hump."

Sky didn't answer; she didn't want to jinx it. She'd heard what Frank had said about lucky charms and sugar pills. Placebos, he'd called them. But she wasn't sure yet.

The filly kept getting stronger, though, standing for longer and longer periods of time. So a couple of nights later, Dr. Nash announced that the next day, they'd put her in with her dam.

"She's coming back to you," Sky told Poppy before she left. "You'll have her back tomorrow."

30

Sky usually dozed on the way back to Shaughnessy, tired from getting up so early, from working all day long. But tonight she was wide awake.

"Poppy will be so happy," she was saying to Frank. "It'll be so good for them both to be together."

"That's for sure." Frank nodded.

"I wish it was tomorrow already! I don't know how I'm going to sleep."

"Count horses," he said. But right away he caught himself. "No, that's wrong." Shaking his head in the dark. "Don't want to count horses this year. All those foals . . ."

Five hundred.

He didn't say it out loud, didn't have to.

When they pulled into Shaughnessy, Sky asked Frank to drop her at the foaling barn.

"I guess I want to check the desk," she said without looking across the seat. "See if there are more packages."

"There are," Frank told her. "Three."

Gaby was busy making last rounds, and normally Sky would've gone to help, but she headed straight to the office. There were three envelopes on the desk, just like Frank had said, which meant three different birds.

A chickadee—at least that's what it looked like. Fat little belly, tail feathers square in the back.

A blue jay—the crown and the way it stood so upright was unmistakable.

A woodpecker—tiny claws up high for grabbing on to the side of a tree, head turned slightly like it was listening.

Sky lined the birds up on the desk and stared at them like they were going to come alive, flutter their wings, and fly away. She turned the envelopes over and studied the postmarks, and her heart rose up inside her chest.

After her father had left, she'd believed deep down that he'd gone back to the ocean, to the place her mother had loved. It hadn't mattered what the note had said, what Frank had told her. Deep down she'd believed he wouldn't come back. She'd been afraid he was gone for good, just like her mother.

Now Sky tossed the envelopes into the trash like she'd done before. But when she opened the drawer, she didn't put the new birds away straight off. She took out the older letters and shuffled them together with the three new ones.

There were dates along the top, she noticed, and she put the letters in order. And then she sat there and read each one, start to finish.

When she was done, she folded them up again and put them back into the drawer. She was still angry, still sad. But she understood a little more about why her father had gone away. She understood how he hadn't gone very far after all and that he'd be back soon. She just had to be patient.

31

Sometimes a mare will reject a foal if they haven't been together from the beginning. Dr. Nash kept worrying about it as they got the filly ready to meet Poppy. But Sky knew nothing like that was going to happen.

You are mine.

That's basically what Poppy kept saying as they brought the filly in.

You are mine.

Nose to nose. Breathing in her scent. Nickering softly. Nudging the filly closer.

I am yours.

The response from Poppy's gal: allowing herself to be poked and prodded in the gentlest way possible, doing a little curious poking back.

I am home.

The filly sank to the ground after the greeting—she couldn't stand for long on her spindly legs. So Poppy moved closer, positioned herself directly over her babe, gentle but firm. She would not let humans take the filly again, that was clear.

"This is great!" Dr. Nash whispered. "Just amazing!"

Everybody watched as Poppy started licking the filly all over—the way any mare will do right after birth—as if no time had passed.

The filly loved the attention. Sky could feel the warmth moving through her, liquid like hot tea, all the way to the points of her tiny hooves.

"I'll come back in about half an hour and we'll stand her up again, try to get her to nurse," Dr. Nash said.

After the vet had gone, Sky moved in close, talking low, explaining how the filly had been fed up until this point. She'd told all this to Poppy before, but she went over it again.

Frank came in a little later, and when Dr. Nash returned, they worked together to lift the filly, to steady her while Poppy moved in close. Sky tugged gently on her udders, getting some milk on her fingers, offering it to the filly, giving her the scent.

"This is where the good stuff is," Sky told her. "This is where you need to get it, not from the bottle."

The filly reached her neck up, stretching as far as she could. Sky knelt down and held the teat for her, making sure her tongue was doing what it was supposed to do.

"That's right, that's right," Sky murmured, and Poppy shifted, making room.

The filly tried—Sky could feel her trying with all her skimpy might, and she was proud of her. Sky could feel the need and the way the taste of milk from her mama, not from a rubber nipple, gave her a tiny jolt. But her legs were so weak. Frank and the vet held her standing as long as they could, and then they eased her down.

"She's done for now," Sky announced.

"It was a good first try," Dr. Nash said, and Frank agreed.

"A darn good first try."

Dr. Nash had one of the assistants come and pump the rest of Poppy's milk so it wouldn't go to waste. Sky settled in with the filly on the floor near the wall, and after a few minutes they handed her the bottle.

"It's okay," she told Poppy. "This is not forever."

Poppy started licking the filly again when she took the bottle, and it made a difference. The filly took more than usual.

"She'll get fat that way," Frank muttered roughly, sounding for all the world like the old cranky Frank.

"Good," Sky threw back. "I want her to get fat. Fat and sassy."

Frank went off to see about the other mares, and after hovering a bit, Dr. Nash and the assistant left too. Poppy licked at Sky some along with the filly.

"Thanks," Sky said. "I could probably use a good cleaning."

She leaned her head back against the wall and closed her eyes. The filly was deep asleep already, and her dreams weren't much—which made sense to Sky. The poor thing hadn't lived any yet, hadn't experienced anything except the hospital with its sterile stalls. She hadn't gone out into a field the way a foal her age would normally be doing by now. She hadn't exploded into a run for no good reason except that she could.

"You will," Sky whispered, knowing it was against every superstition she'd ever been taught, knowing she couldn't help it. "You will."

32

A late frost hit just when they least expected it, just like Frank had predicted way back at the beginning of the crazy early spring. Sky awoke before dawn, and the world was dusted white, sparkling. She made her way out of Frank's cottage, white breath puffing out, boots crunching brittle grass.

Sky stopped and leaned over to see what else was crunching beneath her feet.

Tiny frozen bodies, curled in tight circles, stiff to the touch, lifeless.

"Are you sad?" she asked Archie when he came to the barn later. "Sad about all the caterpillars dying?"

He shook his head. "Circle of life, like I said before. Plus I *was* able to save a few in the aquariums."

"Great. Bug TV, continued." She put her hand on his arm. "Do me a favor, though?"

"What?"

"Don't do the usual catch and release. I'm glad the caterpillars are gone now. I'm sorry, but I just am."

Archie nodded; he knew what she meant, even if he did love bugs. There was no proof that the caterpillars had anything to do with the foals dying. But Sky thought there had to be a connection—they'd had a plague of caterpillars and then a plague of death. Sky believed there had to be a connection, and Archie couldn't say anything that could contradict that.

The mail came right before Sky left for Bright and Butler— two more envelopes from her father—and Frank waited inside the office while she opened them.

The birds were painted this time—a brown robin with its bright red breast, and a small yellow bird, familiar, though Sky couldn't remember its name.

"A goldfinch," Frank told her when she held it up for him to see.

"A goldfinch," Sky repeated.

She read the letters, then tucked them away with the others. She was silent in the car while they drove, thinking about her father.

"He's getting better," Frank said, guessing what—who— was on her mind.

"At carving?" she asked.

"At everything."

Sky thought about that for a moment. "How do you know?"

Frank threw a stern look her way. "I talk to him, of course."

"But he left his phone in his room."

"Yeah, and there are no other phones in the world." Frank gave her another look, one bushy eyebrow raised this time. And Sky realized that the old man knew what was in one of the letters: a phone number. Her father had told her to call when she was ready. But she wasn't ready, not yet.

When they got to Bright and Butler, Sky began in Poppy's stall. The filly was wonderfully alert, teetering around the space on her skinny legs, curious like a foal should be. The sight gave Sky strength to move on to Juniper's stall.

Juniper's filly had taken a sharp turn for the worse, hadn't made it after all. So Frank was getting the mare ready to trailer back to Shaughnessy. He'd be taking Callabee and Circe, too. Both mares had delivered stillborns.

"Your friends are waiting," Sky told each of the mares in turn. "And you'll have Gaby and the whole of Shaughnessy to pamper you, that's for sure. All the best hay, the best oats, everything you could wish for."

Next Sky went to see Shaker Rose, whose colt had been

born puny and weak, just like Poppy's filly, but had had a stronger drive to suck, so he'd started nursing a lot quicker and was gaining weight at a faster rate. His ears weren't floppy at all.

Besides the Shaughnessy Two, as the vets called them, there were a few more foals from other farms.

"Quite the nursury we've got," Dr. Nash kept saying, and Sky could tell she was thrilled even though she kept her voice flat and professionial.

Dr. Nash was the youngest on staff, and Sky noticed that sometimes the older vets tried to boss her, just like they were all horses in a herd. But Dr. Nash was the favorite as far as the mares were concerned—the one they trusted the most—and so she was Sky's favorite too.

In fact, Sky started making rounds with her—unofficial, of course. Sky would be sitting in Poppy's or Shaker Rose's stall, and Dr. Nash would walk by and mention she was going to see a new mare that had just been admitted, would Sky care to join her?

As long as the Shaughnessy mares didn't need her, the answer was always yes and Sky would tag along to the other stalls, visit with the mares who still had sickly foals as well as the mares who'd "dropped" but still had issues that kept them in the hospital.

Meeting other horses from other farms meant that Sky could add to the notes she'd made in the little black book Archie had given her. She could try to connect what all the mares had in common.

Prickly. Stings. Tongue too big. Hard to swallow. More stinging.

The memory was mostly the same, whether it was Poppy or Valeria, who came from Majestic Farms, all the way across two counties.

"Is that a journal you're keeping?" Dr. Nash asked one day when she saw Sky scribbling in the book between stalls.

"Sort of," Sky answered, hesitating, trying to decide whether or not to show Dr. Nash what she'd written.

Would she believe Sky? Or would she just laugh?

"It's just some thoughts about . . . horses," Sky added, shoving the book in her back pocket.

Dr. Nash nodded knowingly. "I used to write poems about horses when I was about your age. And draw pictures. I've always been crazy for horses."

"Me too," Sky said, and left it at that—for now.

"I think she'd understand," Archie told her when she was back at the barn, going over the day with him. "From how you've described her, she seems like the kind of person who would understand." He glanced up. "I did."

33

Maybe she did it on purpose, leave the little black book on the bench in the room where the women changed into scrubs. Maybe she knew Dr. Nash would find it and not just return it but glance through it first, maybe even stop and read more carefully.

"I hope you don't think I'm nosy," Dr. Nash said, holding the book out to her in front of Poppy's stall, "but you've made a lot of interesting observations about a lot of different horses."

"Thanks," Sky said, tucking the book to her chest.

Dr. Nash nearly turned away, but then she stopped. "It's not really my place," she said, "but you're obviously extra-ordinarily gifted. I think you'd make a great vet when you're older. You might want to think about that."

Sky was surprised. She'd only ever thought of following in her father's footsteps, working on different farms, following the horse circuit. She'd never thought about doing some-thing so . . . permanent.

"Could I work just with horses?" Sky asked.

"Oh, yes, of course!" Dr. Nash answered. "That's what I do, what all of us here do. It could be your specialty."

Sky nodded. "Maybe I'll think about it."

"Well, of course that's a long way off, but it's something to consider. Because you're so good with horses. You really care about them, and you're smart." She reached out and tapped the notebook. "All those notes, they're great, lots of observations, ideas." She seemed to hesitate, but then went ahead. "The only thing I'd say is that you have to be really objective. As a vet, as a scientist. If you're trying to find the reason behind something, like MRLS, you have to try to be objective and just take notes on what you observe, what you actually see. Not on what you imagine the subject—the horse—feels."

Sky kept the black book against her chest. Now would be the time. She could just throw it out there and see what happened.

I can talk to horses. I can speak their language.

But the moment passed. Another vet called for Dr. Nash, and she gave Sky a pat on the shoulder, then turned to deal with some other case.

A few more mares were admitted that day, and Dr. Nash told Sky to go on and visit them on her own because she'd gotten tied up with lots of paperwork.

Arabesque was a famous broodmare from Cheshire Farms. Sky had read about her in trade papers, heard her name spoken by the Macs once or twice. She was the same age as Lady Blue. In fact they'd often raced together, Sky discovered after she'd talked with her for a while. Arabesque and Lady Blue had a lot in common—the same number of foals, all succesful births with only one loss—this year's.

They had something else in common too.

Prickly. Stings. Tongue too big. Hard to swallow. More stinging.

Sky listened as Arabesque told her a similar story to the one she'd heard from her mares, from so many others. And then she went on to the next stall and the next, and it was all the same.

Prickly. Stings. Tongue too big. Hard to swallow. More stinging.

It couldn't be a coincidence; Sky was sure of it.

So she went to Dr. Nash's office and waited for her, biting her lip the whole time, biting the inside of her cheek, which had finally started to heal. Sky kept checking her watch—Frank would come looking for her soon to go back to Shaughnessy for evening chores—but Dr. Nash never came.

Finally, before Sky could lose her nerve, she tore a piece of paper out of the book and wrote Dr. Nash a note. Then she set it all on her desk, on top of everything, so the vet would be sure to see it.

Halfway down the hall, Sky had second thoughts. She nearly dashed back, grabbed what she'd left. But she thought about everything she'd learned, the connections she'd made to so many different horses. It had to mean something, it *had* to. And she couldn't keep it a secret just because she was afraid people would think she was crazy.

Sky was able to talk to horses; she was able to speak their language. And if admitting that would help at all with finding out what had killed the foals—what was still killing them—then she couldn't stay quiet.

34

The grass in Kentucky isn't really blue. It's a name, a type. But Sky's mother used to pretend anyway after a long day of driving from one job to the next.

"Look it! The grass is blue!" she'd cry, pointing out the window of the truck toward the moving fields.

"No, it's not," Sky would scoff, acting the grown-up.

"Oh, you're right. The grass is purple."

"There's no such thing as purple grass!"

"Hold on a minute. Maybe it's pink. What do you think, James?"

"Pink," Sky's father would say, making a show of squinting out the window. "Definitely a pink tinge there."

"And what would happen if the horses ate pink grass?" Sky would demand.

"Well, maybe they'd turn pink themselves!" her mother

answered in her quick way. "Maybe the pink grass would make them turn pink."

Sky shook her head firmly and turned to her father. She always sat in the front seat, right in between them. That's how they always traveled.

"Have you ever seen pink horses?" she asked.

"Hmmmm . . . can't say that I have, but you never know, I s'pose."

"Flamingos!" Her mother snapped her fingers, eyes wide. "Flamingos turn pink because they eat so much shrimp!" She'd open her hands as if that explained everything. "So if a horse ate pink grass and nothing else all day long, she'd turn pink herself."

"Maybe you're right, Maggie May."

That's what her father always called her mother. Maggie May. Sky's mother would often say she was really just plain old Margaret from Albany, New York, but once she'd met James Doran, she became Maggie May.

"Oh, look it! There's a pink horse now!" her mother said then, pointing out the window.

And Sky would look. She'd look and look, and she'd almost believe she saw a pink horse just because her mother said it was there.

The memory came to Sky as she held the tiny pink

flamingo in the palm of her hand—a new bird her father had sent.

The memory was one of a hundred that she hadn't gone back to since her mother had died, hadn't let herself go back to. Because it hurt too much.

Another: How her mother had loved telling the story of Sky's birth, the reason she'd named her daughter Sky. Because that's what Maggie May was looking at when the baby was born. Not some hospital room ceiling—not any kind of ceiling at all, except the one that covers the whole world.

Another: How a week before her mother died they'd been walking on the beach—slow and careful because Maggie May was so weak by then, so tiny, her strong body whittled down to nearly nothing.

"Look it!" her mother cried, pointing to something sticking up in the sand.

It was a sand dollar. Bone white, nearly perfect. Just one tiny nick at the top.

"Lots of luck," her mother said. "Finding nearly a whole one like this. A lifetime's worth."

Her mother held the sand dollar in her hand for a moment, and then she gave it to Sky, setting it lightly in her palm, closing Sky's fingers gently around it.

"Keep it safe, my darling girl," her mother whispered. "Keep it always."

And Sky promised she would, but she didn't.

A couple of days after her mother died, she took the sand dollar from its place on her bedroom shelf in the trailer. She put it on the floor and smashed it with the heel of her boot, smashed it to bits. She couldn't stand that her mother had given her all the luck when she was the one who'd needed it most of all.

Sky gazed at what was resting in her hand right now. The flamingo. For some reason she'd thought her father would stick with Kentucky birds. And maybe he should have.

This bird wasn't as fine as the last few had been, wasn't as detailed. Sky knew it was a flamingo because of the stilt legs, the long feathers, the pink paint. Because of the memory.

In the letters she'd finally read, her father had told her about the table he sat at while he did his whittling—a big picture window looking out over the grounds. He told her about the special knives and the paints they let him use. He told her about the room—the Craft Room, it was called. He told about some of the other guys he'd become friends with, even a few horse people among them: a jockey, a trainer, the son of a big-deal horse family, as rich and well known as the

Macs, all of them with some kind of problem they hadn't been able to kick on their own. Drugs mostly, but drinking too, like her father. All of them there for thirty days at least to get clean, to get sober, to get straight. Like her father.

He told her about the place: the Lexington Rehabilitation Center. Not very far at all. About thirty minutes from where she was sitting. The call wouldn't even be long distance.

Sky put the flamingo into the drawer with the other birds and pulled out the letters, shuffled through them until she found the one with the number. She still felt angry; she still felt confused. But she didn't want to keep it to herself anymore. She wanted to tell her father, and she wanted to listen, too. So she picked up the phone on the desk and started to dial.

35

She didn't really try to avoid Dr. Nash when she got to Bright and Butler. But she didn't go looking for her either. She stayed with Poppy and the filly mostly, then Shaker Rose and the colt.

There were a lot of emergencies that day. Sky kept hearing Dr. Nash's name being paged over the intercom. When she finally stopped into Poppy's stall, it was near the end of the day.

"She's doing really well," Sky blurted immediately, afraid of what Dr. Nash might say. "I think she wants to get out of this stall soon. I think she wants to run. Her legs are stronger. She's definitely put some meat on her bones."

"Awesome," Dr. Nash said, though her voice sounded more tired than usual. When Sky looked up, she noticed dark circles under the vet's eyes, and her short hair was sticking up at odd angles like she hadn't brushed it in a while.

"Hard day?" Sky asked.

"Just busy," Dr. Nash answered, picking up the chart and glancing through it. "Nonstop for a while. But nothing really serious. Nothing to do with MRLS, for a change."

"That's good." Sky went back to what she'd been doing before Dr. Nash had arrived—pushing an exercise ball and watching the filly sniff at it, push at it with her nose, startle when it rolled away. The hospital used the balls—big, soft rubber balls—to help with a foal's sense of balance, sense of play.

"Did she finish up her second feeding today?" Dr. Nash asked.

"She sure did. She was hungry!"

Dr. Nash went through all the usual questions, checking things off as Sky answered. Nothing seemed out of the ordinary, and so Sky realized that her note, her book, must have gotten lost under a pile of new cases, which meant that Dr. Nash hadn't even seen it!

In a way, Sky was disappointed. But in another way, she was relieved. When Sky had finally spoken to her father on the phone, she hadn't mentioned anything about this, about telling their secret. She'd explained what she was doing at Bright and Butler, what she was helping with. Her father had been so proud, she hadn't wanted to blurt out the rest of it.

"Wonderful progress," Dr. Nash said, tapping her pen on the chart. "Really terrific."

Sky nodded in agreement. She thought about how Dr. Nash would probably go on to Shaker Rose's stall next. Maybe she could pretend she had to use the bathroom but really duck into Dr. Nash's office. She could grab the black book and take it back. In a day or two, she'd find another way to tell about the stinging on the tongues, the prickly feeling. She'd say that she suddenly remembered seeing cuts from way back, from before the mares started foaling—could that mean anything?

"Looks like the techs weighed her this morning, and she's put on another two pounds," Dr. Nash was saying. "And her temperature is staying steady and her lungs are clear."

"She's doing great," Sky agreed. She glanced at the door, ready to get on with her plan.

"Yes, I can *see* she's doing great," Dr. Nash began. "But I guess what I really want to know is how she's actually *feeling*, what she's actually *thinking*."

Sky stared at the vet.

"Yes, I've read your note," Dr. Nash said, closing the chart. "And I admit I'm a little skeptical. I mean, it's not something we're trained to believe in. Talking to animals. As a vet, it's not very . . ."

"Logical," Sky finished the sentence for her. "Scientific," she added, and then she started laughing, she couldn't help it.

Dr. Nash cocked her head, confused, so Sky hurried to explain.

"A friend of mine says the exact same thing. He wants to be an entomologist. He likes bugs more than horses. But I like him anyway. He believes me, believes what I can do."

"Ah, I see." Dr. Nash smiled. Sky could tell that she didn't really see but that she was trying to, and that meant a lot.

"What you wrote in your book," Dr. Nash continued. "It doesn't fit with what I've been taught as a scientist and a veterinarian. In fact, most people wouldn't believe what you're saying. They'd think you were making it all up just to . . . I don't know, get some attention maybe."

"I'm not making it up!" Sky blurted.

Dr. Nash put a hand up. "I can't deny you have a way with horses, Sky. Probably more than anyone I've ever seen. You have an incredible gift."

"Thank you." Sky glanced down to her blue bubble feet.

"I can't deny it would be helpful to have a different perspective on MRLS," Dr. Nash said, "to have the horses actually be able to tell us something, anything, if they could."

"They *can* tell us. They *have* told us. Told *me*," Sky corrected.

"But the cuts in their mouths . . . ," Dr. Nash started. "It just doesn't seem like enough—"

"I know!" Sky interrupted. "Whatever it is, it's not obvious. Because I was there for it all, at least for our mares, and nothing was wrong. Not badly wrong. They weren't sick, they weren't suffering. Except for what I wrote down in the book. Except for those stings they felt on their tongues, those prickles. Those cuts I saw myself."

Dr. Nash pursed her lips. Sky couldn't tell if the vet believed her or not, but she put down the chart and took out a small flip notebook from her coat pocket, clicked open her pen.

"When did you start noticing the cuts?" Dr. Nash asked, and Sky gave her the exact date—she'd pinned it down, memorized it. The vet jotted that down and kept asking more questions. As they went through everything, Sky noticed that Dr. Nash didn't seem so tired anymore. There were still circles under her eyes, but her eyes were bright now, excited. She was full of new energy.

"I want to get the timing straight," she was saying. "And then I want to examine the mares you've . . . *talked* to." She glanced at Sky for confirmation, and Sky nodded. "If it all adds up, I'll send my notes to a scientist I know at the research lab."

"Okay." Sky took a breath. "I'm ready." She'd helped the filly settle down as they were talking, and the foal was sound asleep. But Poppy had stayed alert, listening to everything.

"We're going to get to the bottom of this," Sky told her. "I promise."

Dr. Nash had moved to the gate and started to open it, but paused.

"I was wondering . . ." She let the sentence trail off. She seemed embarrassed.

"What?" Sky asked.

"Oh, I guess it's silly, but I suppose I want to know what the horses think of me." She shrugged. "I know that being a vet isn't a popularity contest, but I've always felt a connection with horses, and I was wondering if that connection was real. If they felt the same way. If they . . . like me as much as I like them."

"Of course they like you!" Sky cried. "You're their favorite vet."

"Really?" Dr. Nash seemed surprised.

"Really."

"Who's their least favorite?" Dr. Nash asked, but then she waved a hand in the air. "Never mind. Forget I asked that."

Sky laughed. "They like most everybody here. They know

you all mean well. But you're special. The mares have told me so. In fact, they think you have a horse soul."

"A horse soul?"

Sky nodded. "Do you believe in reincarnation?" she asked suddenly.

"I'm not sure," Dr. Nash said. "To be honest, I haven't thought about it that much."

"It's what my mom believed." Sky looked away, then back again. "Anyway, Poppy and the others, they think you have a horse soul. And believe me, that's the highest compliment you can get from a horse."

Dr. Nash blinked a few times. Sky could tell she was on the fence—whether to truly believe or not. Finally, though, something seemed to shift.

"A horse soul," she repeated. "That's really something. Tell them, tell Poppy I'm honored."

"I don't mean to be rude," Sky said, "but you can tell Poppy yourself." She laughed. "I mean, just because you don't understand their language doesn't mean they don't understand yours."

Dr. Nash's eyes went wide again. She looked exactly like the little girl Sky had mistaken her for on that first night.

"Of course." The doctor shook her head. She looked at Poppy, and Poppy looked back with her big, knowing eyes.

"I'm honored," Dr. Nash told her. "Thank you."

You are welcome.

That's what Poppy answered. And Sky knew Dr. Nash *understood* even if she couldn't *hear* exactly.

36

After that day, a lot of things happened, one right on top of the other.

The first thing was that Dr. Nash—or Jo Ellen, Jo as she told Sky to call her since they'd be spending so much time together—took down her own notes based on the little black book. She examined all the mares she could. Then she wrote a report and emailed it to her scientist friend at the research lab.

The scientist emailed back right away and said all this new "data," as he called it, was fascinating, that it supported a letter he'd gotten recently.

"A letter?" Sky asked.

"Yes," Jo said, reading from her computer screen. "Apparently a man named James Doran wrote to the lab as well. Mentioned a bunch of cuts he and his daughter noticed on the tongues of the mares they were caring for." She looked up. "Any relation?"

"That's my dad!" Sky cried, as if Jo hadn't figured that part out herself.

"He's been in a rehab center all this time," Sky continued. "That's why . . . um . . . that's why he hasn't been here with me, that's why I've just been with Frank. My dad has a problem—a drinking problem. I didn't know about it before because he'd stopped the day he met my mom, the day he fell in love with her. But then she died last winter. She died of cancer." Sky paused, swallowing. "And it was really hard, and it made him start drinking again. It made him a different person . . . a different person than he really was. So he had to go away. But he's getting better and then he'll be back."

Sky stopped, breathless. She hadn't known she was going to say all that. She was surprised. And so was Jo.

"Oh my goodness," Jo said, and Sky hoped against hope that she wasn't going to just say "sorry," so Sky would have to just say "thanks."

"You've had to deal with a lot, haven't you, Sky? A whole lot. More than most kids your age."

Sky was about to shrug it off like it was nothing, but she didn't. Because it wasn't.

"Yeah," she said finally. "I guess I have. But I'm strong. Really strong. I know that now."

"I know it too," Jo said.

The second thing that happened was that they got to bring the mares and the foals back home. The filly and colt had grown strong enough, and so Sky helped truck them all back to the weanling barn, to the special stalls they'd prepared, and gave them a grand homecoming party that everybody on the farm attended, of course.

"I'm so happy! I couldn't be happier!" Mrs. Mac kept saying over and over again, knocking the air out of Sky every single time she said it by wrapping her into an extra, extra tight hug.

"Better you than me," Archie whispered. But Sky got him back by mentioning on the next hug that she thought her grandson looked like he could use one too. And then it was Archie she was squeezing the living daylights out of.

"Now I know what a caterpillar must feel like when it's trapped inside its cocoon, waiting to be a butterfly," he whispered to Sky, scrunching up his face.

"Good," she told him, grinning from ear to ear. "All in the name of science."

* * *

The third thing of course was that James Doran came back to Shaughnessy, back to Sky.

She almost didn't recognize him at first, walking down the aisle of the weanling barn: dark hair cut shorter than Sky had ever seen, cropped close to his head, which made the gray more visible. But that didn't matter. He'd filled out some, especially in the face—shaven and smooth. His clothes weren't hanging like scarecrow rags anymore. He looked strong, as strong as he'd been before.

"I have a new bird for your collection," he said, holding his arm out, fist closed so she couldn't see it at first.

"What kind is it?" Sky asked, taking a step closer.

"See for yourself." His hand opened then, palm out flat. "See if I got it right."

The bird could've been a seagull. It had the same white muscular body as a gull, the same long white wings—spread out of course, poised in flight. The beak and feet were bright orange, and there was a circle of black at the top of its head. A jaunty black beret—that's how her mother used to describe it.

"An arctic tern," Sky whispered. "It's perfect."

Her father came closer. "Your mom told me how they fly the most. More than any other bird." Carefully he placed the carving in Sky's hand. "They fly everywhere—across the whole wide world."

"I know," she said, and her fingers closed around the bird, holding it tight.

"I'm sorry, luv," James Doran told her then. "So very sorry." And then he took her in his arms, held her fast. "I'm sorry I ran away. From everything, from you. But I won't ever do it again. I'm here now, I promise."

Sky nodded against his shoulder. Because she knew. The words weren't just floating around inside her own head. The words were real; the words were true. And they were exactly what she'd been waiting for.

Epilogue

It's a rule that every foal turns one year old on January 1, no matter when they were actually born.

Normally Sky would never be around when the colts and fillies officially became yearlings at Shaughnessy. She'd be in Florida with her mother and father, sitting between them like always on a warm beach, gazing out across the water, watching a bunch of dolphins—if they were lucky—leap and dive in the far-off waves.

Of course nothing about that year was normal.

And so here Sky was, bundled up to her eyeballs on a freezing New Year's morning in Kentucky, watching two gangly yearlings—who didn't seem to feel the cold at all—tag each other back and forth across a frosty field.

"At least it's sunny," Archie observed, the words muffled by the scarf wrapped around his head.

"Thank goodness for small favors." Something Frank always said.

"Plus we've got some hot chocolate Grams packed." Archie started rummaging around in his backpack—awkward work with all his layers and thick gloves—and came up with a thermos for each of them.

"Thank goodness for Mrs. Mac," Sky revised, taking her leather covers off and stuffing them into her coat pocket, leaving the liners on and holding the thermos between her palms to draw the warmth.

"I bet the cold was a shock when you got off the plane," she said.

"A little different from what I'm used to," he agreed.

"I guess it's pretty hot there?"

"It can be," Archie said. He lived in Uganda now with his parents—in Kampala. They'd found a home, a local school Archie liked. They'd be there a couple of years at least, then probably move to a new post. But they'd all come back to Shaughnessy for Christmas.

Archie had talked nonstop about bugs since he'd arrived, shown Sky millions of pictures he'd taken around Kampala, but also on trips he'd gone on with his parents outside the city—to the nature preserves and rain forests and even the desert. Photos of giant horned beetles and shaggy spiders

and a centipede nearly as long and fat as her forearm—
which crawled right into a nightmare or two.

"Africa truly is bug heaven for Archie," Mrs. Mac had
whispered to Sky just last night at dinner, and they'd both
given big fake shudders, laughing all the while.

"It takes some time to adjust to the heat," Archie was saying now. "But your body adapts. You get used to it. We're a
highly adaptable species, you know. Humans."

"I guess we are," Sky replied, taking a tentative sip from
the thermos.

At Shaughnessy, they'd all had to adapt to caring for two
foals instead of the standard fifty-two. They'd had to adjust
what they usually ordered for the year; less hay, less straw,
less grain and supplies.

They'd had to adjust what they usually expected of the
foals, the typical milestones. When to wean and when to
separate. When to start the training that might put one or
more of the foals on the path to being a champion racehorse,
maybe even a Kentucky Derby winner.

Poppy's filly and Shaker Rose's colt would probably never
race. They were small for their age, stunted. In the beginning
they were both prone to sickness. Their lungs would fill with
fluid on and off, and Sky and her father would have to bring
them back to Bright and Butler for treatment.

They were healthy now, healthy as horses, Frank liked to say. But they'd never grow as big or as strong as their dams.

Sky's father had decided to wean the pair late since it had taken them so long to get the hang of nursing in the first place. And he hadn't separated them either. Both were too big to be in their mamas' stalls, so they'd been given their own—always side by side in the barn, though, always turned out together. A happy foursome.

Poppy and Shaker Rose were out there now, proud mamas. Not too close to the pair to seem like they were hovering, but near enough if anything went amiss.

"What are we going to name these two?" Mr. Mac had asked when they first brought them home to Shaughnessy from the hospital. Nobody had wanted to name them before, at Bright and Butler. Nobody had wanted to get their hopes that high.

But once they came back home, the pair needed to be named.

"The missus and I have discussed it," Mr. Mac told Sky then. "We'd like you to do the honors."

Grace.

Wonder.

The names came to Sky right away. And they mostly had to do with the foals' personalities.

Poppy's filly was calm and still, and she made Sky feel calm and still herself.

Shaker Rose's colt was the opposite. He was always asking questions inside his head, questions about crickets and trees and floating leaves, questions only Sky and her father could hear. He was always poking around, sniffing at things, looking at the world with even wider horse eyes than usual, curious and amazed by everything at once.

Sky had said the names out loud that first day back, and everybody thought they were perfect. Later she typed them into the computer log, two full names among all those lost and labeled "Dropped."

Poppy's Grace.

Wonder of Shaker Rose.

"I'm glad it's been a cold winter," Sky said to Archie now. They'd finished the hot chocolate and he was putting the thermoses away. "All the bad stuff gets frozen out."

"Caterpillars aren't bad. Or good, for that matter. They just . . . are."

"I know, I know." Sky rolled her eyes. "But if we'd had the same kind of winter last year, this kind of cold, if . . ." She stopped then, let it go.

"If" is a small word, but big enough to drive you mad.

That's what Frank liked to say.

"Well, even *if* the cold wasn't freezing things out, there wouldn't be any caterpillars around anyway. Gramps would make sure of that," Archie said. "Cut down trees, spray pesticides. He's become almost as obsessed by bugs as I am, though not for the same reasons. But I suppose I should be glad we have something in common now. He's actually interested when I show him my photos."

Sky nodded. It was true Mr. Mac talked about caterpillars a lot. He'd go with Frank to check around all the edges of the farm, make sure there were no wild cherry trees. He'd personally gone to the state highway department and gotten them to cut down the ones on the main roads.

"You can't blame your gramps for wanting to kill caterpillars," Sky said, "once we found out that's what was to blame."

Jo had come by the farm to tell the Dorans in person, before the lab announced its findings officially.

The terrible outbreak of MRLS *was* caused by caterpillars—because there'd been so many, because the mares couldn't avoid eating them while they grazed. It wasn't because of the cyanide in their bodies, though, like everybody thought at first. It was because the prickly bits of the caterpillars caused cuts on the tongues like those Sky had seen. The prickles had caused cuts farther down too, deep inside the mares' throats.

The cuts weren't very big, but they were deep enough to let infection in at just the wrong time. Infection grew without it ever showing, without anyone ever knowing. The infection wasn't strong enough to hurt the mares, but it was something most of the unborn foals simply could not survive.

The information Sky and her father had given had helped. It was one piece of a very big puzzle. Their names were listed at the end of some long paper that had been published in veterinary and science journals about MRLS.

But none of that mattered to Sky, not really. What mattered now was making sure it never happened again.

"Hey, I've got something for you," Sky said to Archie.

She reached into her coat pocket and pulled out a little wooden horse. Not the very first she'd tried—she'd kept that for herself. But a new one, just for Archie.

She'd been carving a lot lately. In fact she'd taken over Gaby's orders from Shakertown once Gaby had left for the season—to backpack around Australia. ("Lots of hunky guys 'down under'!")

Sky had actually made a fair amount of pocket money with her horse carvings before Christmas. And her father had kept carving birds, too, all kinds, tiny but detailed as anything. The Dorans would sit together at night and whittle, and they would talk about Maggie May, talk about her until it seemed like she was right there with them.

"It's cherry wood from the farm," Sky explained now, handing it over. "Not wild black cherry, just regular cherry. From a tree we cut down last fall."

"Thanks," Archie said. He took off a glove so he could touch it properly. "It's so smooth! And the horse looks so real." He glanced over at her. "You've gotten really good at this."

"Thanks." She studied her boots. Her jeans weren't high-waters anymore. She'd grown another inch at least—she was still taller than Archie—but she had clothes that fit her now.

"Anyway," Sky said, "I thought you'd like to have a bit of Shaughnessy with you, no matter where you are, in Africa or wherever." Sky laughed. "Seeing as how you're the one traveling now. You're the one without a *real* home."

Archie grinned at that. He studied the horse a while longer before tucking it carefully into his coat pocket. "How does it feel, anyway?"

"To be a rooter?" Sky asked, and when he seemed confused, she explained. "That's what Dad says his granny called it—when you settle somewhere, put down roots."

"Rooter," Archie repeated the word. "I like the sound of that. Do you?"

Sky glanced across to the mares who were trying to find something to nibble despite the frost. She loved seeing Poppy every day, grooming and riding her, loved talking to her all the time.

She liked being with the Macs too, and Frank of course. Even though he'd gotten his bark back—with a vengeance. But he needed Sky and her father more than before, needed the help around the farm. The terrible foaling season had aged him, even if he didn't like to admit it.

"Yeah," Sky said. "I do like being a rooter." She took in a lung full of frigid air and gave a grin. "At least for now."

Sky and Archie stood for a while longer without talking. The warmth from the hot chocolate was wearing off, so Sky decided there was only one thing left to do.

"Come on, race you!" Sky shouted, and then she took off fast without waiting for Archie to say yes or no.

She ran straight for the yearlings, who'd stopped to poke their heads at something in the brittle grass.

"No fair!" Sky heard Archie shout behind her, and she knew he'd started running too, but she didn't turn to check.

Sky kept going, straight for the pair, and their heads startled up when she came into their view—the mamas looking up too—and the young ones took a couple of prancing steps like they were winding a spring inside their bodies.

And the second that spring released, they were gone, flashing a gorgeous reddish brown across the field, disappearing in the blink of an eye.

And even though Sky kept running, kept trying to catch up, she knew she never would, not in a million years.

The yearlings might be small on this, their very first official birthday, they might never race for fame or fortune. But none of that mattered one little bit.

Grace and Wonder were alive and running, running faster than the wind itself. Running just because they could, because that's what a horse is born to do.

Author's Note

This is not a true story, but part of it was inspired by real and tragic events.

In and around the year 2001, over five hundred Thoroughbred foals died in broodmare farms across the state of Kentucky. Some foals never came to full term; some were stillborn. A few foals did survive, but they were often sickly and needed constant care.

The loss of so many foals in one season was devastating to the Kentucky Thoroughbred industry, and of course it was heartbreaking to horse lovers everywhere. As in this story, many volunteers from around the state and the region came to help.

The foal epidemic was quickly given a name: Mare Reproductive Loss Syndrome, or MRLS. But what caused MRLS remained a mystery for a long time—longer than I portray in the book. Scientists and veterinarians at the prestigious Gluck Equine Research Center at the University of Kentucky in Lexington actually worked for several years to find a reason and a cure.

The eastern tent caterpillar was a suspect from the beginning because, after an unusually mild winter, there had been a huge infestation that spring. It truly was a "plague of caterpillars," as Mrs. Mac says in the book. And in the end, the reason behind MRLS truly was something seemingly simple: Tiny cuts from grazing on so many caterpillars had caused infections either too early or too late in mare pregnancies for foals to develop the immunity they needed in order to survive.

As far as I know, there was no one person (like Sky Doran) who ultimately helped connect the dots and solve the MRLS mystery; there was no one girl who talked to horses. But I'm a writer, so I like to imagine that there was . . . or is.

There *are* many horse experts throughout Kentucky, though, and I'd like to acknowledge a few in particular:

Deepest thanks goes to Pete Cline, manager of Shawnee Farm in Mercer County, owned by Sally and Watts Humphrey, and home to some of the most beautiful creatures ever made, not to mention some pretty awe-inspiring green fencing.

Thanks also to Pete's family—Robin, Jack, and Kevin—along with the whole staff at Shawnee Farm, especially assistant manager Wick Hughes and night watchwoman Penny Roney, all of whom patiently answered lots of questions. Without the folks at Shawnee, I never would have known what it's like to be startled awake in the middle of the night by a phone call, to rush out into the cold dark, half awake and wondering if I'd make it in time; I never would have known what it's like to experience for myself the miracle of seeing a healthy foal come into the world.

A special thanks goes to Mary DeLima of DeLima Stables, also in Mercer County, whose knowledge of and patience with horses (and children) has been deeply inspiring over the past few years.

Thanks to Cedars of Peace in Loretto, Kentucky, where significant drafts of this novel were finished in Wonder and in Grace.

As always, extra love goes to my husband, Tim, and my children, Daniel, Lila, and Theo, as well as to my mother, Charlotte. Extra love also goes to my longtime friend and editor, Caitlyn Dlouhy, without whom this book would not be what it is.

Bibliography

Articles

Associated Press. "Plus: Horse Racing; Cyanide Possible Cause of Deaths." *The New York Times*, May 25, 2001. http://www.nytimes.com/2001/05/25/sports/plus-horse-racing-cyanide-possible-cause-of-deaths.html

Clines, Francis X. "A Horse Mystery Puts Kentucky on Edge." *The New York Times*, May 20, 2001. http://www.nytimes.com/2001/05/20/us/a-horse-mystery-puts-kentucky-on-edge.html

Dwyer, Roberta M., Lindsey P. Garber, Albert J. Kane, Barry J. Meade, Michael P. Pavlick, David Powell, and Josie L. Traub-Dargatz. "Case-control study of factors associated with excessive proportions of early fetal losses associated with mare reproductive loss syndrome in central Kentucky during 2001." *Journal of the American Veterinary Medical Association* 222, no. 5 (March 1, 2003): 613-19. doi: 10.2460/javma.2003.222.613.

Graetz, Kimberly S. "Excessive Foal Loss Great Concern to Central Kentucky Farms." *Blood-Horse* magazine, May 7, 2001. https://www.bloodhorse.com/horse-racing/articles/4027

Mead, Andy. "Insects Stage Invasion." *The Lexington Herald-Leader*, May 11, 2009.

Paulick, Ray. "Foal Losses 'Devastating' to Family-Run Jonabell Farm." *Blood-Horse* magazine, May 10, 2001. https://www.bloodhorse.com/horse-racing/articles/4112

Wong, Edward. "Horse Racing; Mystery Illness Hurts Horse Breeding in Kentucky." *The New York Times*, May 10, 2001. http://www.nytimes.com/2001/05/10/sports/horse-racing-mystery-illness-hurts-horse-breeding-in-kentucky.html

Nonfiction Books

Archambeault, James. *Kentucky Horse Country: Images of the Bluegrass.* Lexington: University Press of Kentucky, 2008.

Archambeault, James and Thomas D. Clark. *Kentucky II.* Portland, OR: Graphic Arts Center Publishing Co. 1989.

Fitzgerald, Terrence D. *The Tent Caterpillars.* Cornell Series in Anthropod Biology. Ithaca, NY: Cornell University Press, 1995.

Hayes, Karen E. N. *The Complete Book of Foaling: An Illustrated Guide for the Foaling Attendant.* New York: Howell Book House, 1993.

Hayes, Tim. *Riding Home: The Power of Horses to Heal.* Foreword by Robert Redford. New York: St. Martin's Press, 2015.

Hill, Cherry. *How to Think Like a Horse: The Essential Handbook for Understanding Why Horses Do What They Do.* North Adams, MA: Storey Publishing, 2006.

Lose, M. Phyllis. *Blessed are the Foals.* 2nd ed. New York: Howell Book House, 1998.

Mackay, Nicci. *Spoken in Whispers: The Autobiography of a Horse Whisperer.* New York: Simon & Schuster, 1998.

Masson, Kathryn. *Stables: Beautiful Paddocks, Horse Barns, and Tack Rooms.* Photography by Paul Rocheleau. New York: Rizzoli, 2010.

Pickeral, Tamsin. *The Majesty of the Horse: An Illustrated History.* Photography by Astrid Harrisson. Hauppauge, NY: Barron's Educational Series, 2011.

Richards, Susan. *Chosen by a Horse: A Memoir.* Orlando, FL: Harcourt, 2007.

Roberts, Monty. *The Man Who Listens to Horses: The Story of a Real-Life Horse Whisperer.* New York: Random House, 2009.

Fiction Books

Evans, Nicholas. *The Horse Whisperer.* New York: Delacorte Press, 1995.

Farley, Walter. *The Black Stallion*. Illustrated by Keith Ward. New York: Random House, 1941.

Henry, Marguerite. *Misty of Chincoteague*. Illustrated by Wesley Dennis. New York: Simon & Schuster, 1947.

Richards, Susan. *Horse Fables*. Illustrated by Ann Disalvo. Monterey, KY: Larkspur Press, 1987.

Sewell, Anna. *Black Beauty*. London: Jarrold and Sons, 1877.

Smiley, Jane. *The Horses of Oak Valley Ranch*. New York: Alfred A. Knopf, 2009–2013.

Tesdell, Diana Secker, ed. *Horse Stories*. Everyman's Pocket Classics. New York: Alfred A. Knopf, 2012.